STONEWALL SPEAKS

STONEWALL SPEAKS

Claude Brown

iUniverse, Inc.

New York Lincoln Shanghai

Stonewall Speaks

iUniverse books may be ordered through booksellers or by contacting:

iUniverse
2021 Pine Lake Road, Suite 100
Lincoln, NE 68512
www.iuniverse.com
1-800-Authors (1-800-288-4677)

This is a book of fiction. Names, characters, places and incidents are the product of the author's imagination or are used fictitiously. Any resemblance to actual events, locales, or persons, living or dead, is coincidental.

ISBN: 0-595-34479-8

Printed in the United States of America

CONTENTS

▼

CHAPTER 1

▼

EARLY YEARS

The Army of Virginia shoveled dirt into my grave while I omnisciently watched. I never dreamed of being buried in Richmond. Life's circumstances determined my final resting-place. During my mortal life I would not have thought of having this immortal capability. My storytelling begins after being wounded at Chancellorsville and dying in Richmond's Confederate infirmary. This after life ghost dimension let me understand my life and the lives of my many friends, which was always caught up in battle and war. My life had meaning hidden in the context of the dedicated causes. My life's greatest joys were my children, friends and family.

I can travel back in time to review my early years in Clarksburg, and how my parents, Jonathan and Julia Jackson, succumb to typhoid fever. However I cannot affect historical change preventing my parent's death. It was sad to see Paw struggling so hard with his law business before he contacted typhoid. I would not change the fact that Uncle Nathaniel and Aunt Martha Jackson adopted me. Uncle Nate and Aunt Martha lived on a small farm with a stream running through it, which was the power supply for their gristmill. The gristmill was used to grind corn to cornmeal, which I was given the opportunity to operate. Operating the mill was very specialized work. It required training to operate the mechanical units of the mill. The corn was hand separated from the cob and bucket-fed into a funnel hopper. A hand control valve fed the corn from the hopper into the grinder turning the shelled corn into cornmeal. If the grinder was fed too much corn, it became clogged, and the excess corn had to be removed by hand. Paw charged each customer ten percent of the total weight for grinding the corn. Each time a customer wanted the corn ground it had to be weighed, and the weight recorded. The ten-percent charge was based on the original input corn weight and not on the weight of the cornmeal. We sold the excess corn meal, or it was fed to the hogs.

What I enjoyed most about the hogs was the butchering. It was a major event when a hog was butchered. I always enjoyed seeing all the neighbors gather to help kill the hog. Initially, the hog was shot and placed on a pallet, and my job was to heat the hot water in a large black pot over an open fire. The pot rested on two large rocks, and after the water was hot I ladled it over the dead hog to begin hair removal. Paw and the neighbors used sharpened butcher knives to remove the hair. After the hair was removed from one side, the hog was turned to complete removal from the second side. The hog's hind legs were bound together, and it was hoisted with a rope pulley system to a tree limb above the ground. Once the hog was in position it was gutted, bled, and the entrails removed. I gathered the guts and buried them in a hole. The hog's insides were washed clean, and the hog was divided into selective cuts.

I worked the farm and mill as long as I could remember. Plowing was the most difficult task, and Nathaniel was glad to have me help out with this chore. He always told me the plowing horse would make a man out of me. I didn't understand at that time the meaning of his statements. He said if the plowing mare, Samatha, wasn't working me hard enough that I wouldn't learn to think. He also related that I shouldn't spend my life plowing that horse. I didn't mind the hard work of plowing, but I hated slopping the hogs. The hogs had to be fed twice a day, and it seemed as if they never got enough to eat. Milking the three cows was always fun even in winter. The cow's body heat kept me warm while I milked.

Our only feud with the neighbors started over our hogs escaping from their pen and wandering in the mountains. If I had been in my present state I might have handled the Junkins-Jackson incident differently. It wasn't the first time the hogs escaped and roamed the mountains; however, they usually found their way home at feeding time. One day three of our hogs were found wandering in the Virginia Mountains by the Junkins family. Three Junkins boys came upon the hogs while hunting. They set upon our hogs with their flintlocks killing all of them. After a few days we noticed the hogs had not returned home as usual, so we begin a search for them. After day and a half searching we found the hogs' remains, and we approached the Junkins concerning the killing of our hogs. Since they were the only ones who used those woods for hunting, we theorized that they had killed the hogs. Revisiting the incident lets me know certainly that they killed the hogs. They denied the killings, and Paw cut off communications with Mr. Junkins and our families remained unfriendly.

Albert Junkins owned an adjoining farm, and they also raised hogs and other livestock. The Junkins family consisted of five boys and one girl named Elinor. We attended school with Elinor and the Junkin boys, and our communications were not cut off. One day coming home from school Al Junkins, Jr. yelled, "Missing any hogs lately?" He was the oldest of the Junkins boys.

I replied, "No, but I'm going to collect for 'em ones you killed."

That was the signal for the fight to begin, and I rushed at him with adrenaline flowing. I hit him in the chest with fists and elbows; however, he recovered in time to throw a wild right fist hitting me in the mouth and nose. I felt and tasted the warm blood, and this heightened my excitement for the fight. He threw another fist, and I stepped aside feeling the breeze rush past my face. At this time I had my senses about me, and I threw two left jabs at his nose and mouth bouncing his head back. I followed with a hard right bouncing his head again. I stepped back, and he approached throwing both lefts and rights. Again, I stepped back to avoid being hit, and I jabbed repeatedly again following with another right. I didn't step back until he had repented, and he agreed not to shoot anymore of our hogs.

It was my last year to attend the one room school under the tutelage of Master O'Nagle. I always sat next to Elinor Junkins, and we became friends often studying together. Unlike her brothers she could read, write and cipher efficiently. It was always a contest to see which one of us finished the assignment first. The competition made learning fun for both of us. I had developed a fondness for Elinor during that last year. I could tell then that she had the same feelings for me. She forgave me for beating up her brother over the hogs. She had deep blue eyes and pouty lips, and her black hair flowed to her waist. The school year ended, and Master O'Nagle told Maw and Paw that he had taught me everything he could teach. He related that I needed higher education outside the confines of Clarksburg, Virginia. Maw and Paw were happy to have me home full time now that my schooling in Clarksburg was finished; however, it was time for me to get on with my destiny. My aspirations for a higher education had grown to a decision-making time. My reading ability needed improvement; however, I had a great ability with arithmetic and ciphering. I now know the hard work Sam and me did plowing the fields influenced my decision for higher education.

Maw and Paw's income was insufficient to sent me to college and raise a family. However, I knew an appointment to West Point Military Academy would pay for a college education. Many Virginia boys aspired to become an officer in the military by attending West Point. Paw and I discussed the matter at length, and Paw said he would talk to the family doctor for his recommendations to get me into West Point Academy. Dr. Skaggs' status in the area gave him many political connections for he socialized with many politicians. He contacted a Virginia congressman, John Mason, to acquire his support and recommendations for me to attend the Academy. Mr. Mason told Dr. Skaggs he would recommend me to the academy if I could pass the entrance exam.

Now I know it was the right time for me to attend West Point. Then it was fortuitous timing for me to attend for there was one opening for someone in the western Virginia area. I knew there would be many boys seeking the same education opportunity as me, and I began studying for the competitive entrance exam. I traveled to Charlottesville for the exam. The test results placed me second in the scoring for admissions to West Point from western Virginia. I was heart broken to see my dreams disappear. My only enlightened time after receiving the disappointing news was when I saw Elinor on the street in Clarksburg. She always smiled and asked how I had been. I never mention my disappointment of not being accepted to the Academy. However, the initial appointee succumbed to cholera, and I was given the appointment to the Academy.

I revisit meeting Elinor at the feed store after the appointment. I loaded the wagon with the feed just as Elinor and her Paw arrived. I waved to Elinor and she waved. I immediately engaged her in conversation.

"How are you today?" I inquired of her.

"I'm doing very well," She replied, "and how about yourself?"

It was an opportunity to let her know about my appointment to West Point. "I'm doing really good. I received my appointment to attend West Point Academy. I should be leaving within the month." I notice her Paw wasn't too interested in my good fortune. I guess he had not forgiven me for the beating I gave Al, Jr.

That night I could hardly sleep, my mind drifted from Elinor to West Point. It would be nice to see Elinor again before I left, or maybe I could see her at my Christmas break. My thoughts turned to the academy again, and I wandered what it would be like. I thought about the classmates I would meet, and I resolved to read and study well and not be a failure. I would miss the family, but I knew I was returning in December. The two remaining weeks went fast, and I was able to help with more planting and mill operations. The morning I caught the train I slopped the hogs my last time until the December break.

CHAPTER 2

▼

WEST POINT ACADEMY

After breakfast the family loaded onto the wagon for the train station trip. The sunny June morning displayed the early blooming spring flowers and trees. Everyone rode quietly into Clarksburg anticipating my departure. Paw pulled in front of the train station, and everyone jumped from the wagon while Maw gave me some parting advice. She advised me to wash daily, pray daily and eat well while my brothers and sisters gathered around for a last hug. I would miss everyone, but the drive within me sustained my motivation to leave home. Paw returned from the ticket counter, and we approached the train together. He handed me the train ticket with two dollars, and he told me to change trains in Pittsburgh. The Pittsburgh train change would take me to New York City. He looked at me and spoke.

"Son, be honest, study hard, and always stand your ground."

His lecture ended as soon as it began, and I boarded the train. Nathan and Martha had been good parents to me, and I always tried to be helpful to them. The porter announced dinner later that evening, but I was too excited to eat much so I bought a glass of buttermilk and corn pone for five cents. The buttermilk was unlike the fresh churned buttermilk Maw always made. The corn pone contained too much sugar with little crust. By midnight the train pulled into the Pittsburgh station for a layover until the New York train arrived. I checked the New York ticket and the dollar ninety-five cents in my pocket. At the station I learned it would be three hours before the train would leave for New York. I found a bench in the corner wall and prepared for the wait. The next thing I knew the conductor was yelling.

"All aboard!"

I had fallen asleep. I checked my ticket and money again, and it was all there. I handed the conductor my ticket, and he related that this train would get me close to West Point Academy. The porter seated me next to a young man about my age and manner of dress. He was asleep. He had brown hair and a rough complexion, and he continued to sleep until breakfast. As the porter announced breakfast he stirred.

"Where are we?' he asked.

"On the train to West Point," I replied.

"Who are you?" he asked.

"Thomas Jackson," I said.

"You going to the Point like me?" he inquired again.

"Yes. And who are you?' I inquired.

"My name's Hiram Grant, and I'm from Cincinnati, Ohio," he replied, "Where are you from?"

"Clarksburg, Virginia," I told him.

"So we're going to the academy to become officers and gentlemen," he related. "To date I've never had the opportunity to be a gentleman so I'll give the officer thing a try. Until now I helped my Paw with the tannery business. It's hard work. Paw worked me from daylight to dark until I found a way to escape. You might say West Point got me out of the tannery business."

We proceeded to breakfast, and I was hungry. I found the small dinner the night before had left me hungry for breakfast. I ordered eggs, bacon, biscuits, honey, coffee and sweet milk, and Hiram ordered pork chops, eggs, coffee and some sweet bread. He ate his breakfast as if he hadn't eaten for days, and when I finished my breakfast the porter presented us with the bill. Hiram looked at the bill then at me.

"Could you stake me breakfast until I'm paid at West Point Academy, and I'll pay you back. I don't have any money," he related. Throughout his life it became Hiram's right to depend on and borrow from other people. He never seemed to have any money. Money always eluded him. He was never successful until he wrote his memoirs before his death.

"I guess so," I replied, "you'll have to pay me back."

"Sure I will," he stated.

The bill's total was twenty cents, which left me with one dollar and seventy-five cents.

The train pulled into New York around dinnertime, and I was glad. I thought I'd be paying for our dinner. As we got off the train Hiram slipped around the corner, and he bought a bottle of whiskey from a stranger. The man pulled the bottle from under his belt and handed it to Hiram. Hiram paid the stranger with coins from his pocket, and he hid the bottle in a bag with his belongings. I never mentioned to Hiram that I had witnessed the transaction. We gathered our belongings and asked directions to the academy. The porter told us it was about two miles west on the main road so Hiram and I started walking. After we walked about a mile a wagon pulled by two mules stopped beside us. The driver asked where we were going, and we told him West Point Academy. He welcomed us aboard and delivered us to the Academy gate. It was a magnificent looking school with a gate made of iron with large pillars holding it in place. Sergeant Robert Lee and Master Joshua Bates met us inside the gate. Lee was an exemplary upper classman, and Master Bates was the admission officer. We were escorted inside the admissions building to a large room containing eight other boys.

Robert Lee introduced everyone and explained the demerit system. Master Bastes interrupted at the end of the introduction by announcing that Robert Lee was the first cadet never to receive a demerit in the academy's history. I always found it to be true that Lee was an exemplary leader. The cadets were A. P. Hill, James Butler, George Custer, William Sherman, John Longstreet, Jeb Stuart, William Rosecran, and John Mosby. We were the first of the new arriving cadets for the class of 1843, and we were invited to seat ourselves at dinner. We sat in hardback chairs scattered around the room next to the chair rail. Hiram sat in the most convenient chair, I sat next to him, Butler next to me, Hill next to Butler and the remainder scattered about the room. The Academy and our training entangled our lives from this time forward.

"What is that smell?" inquired Hill.

I didn't think too much about his question. I never notice any smell.

"It's not me smelling," Butler replied.

"It smells like shit," Hill related. "What that on your pants and shoes Tom?"

Before I could answer Hiram spoke, "It's a little hog shit Hill. Haven't you ever smelled hog shit before?" Hiram had worked in his Paw's tannery before coming to the Academy, and he recognized the smell of hog shit. The statement put Hill in his place while James Butler continued to laugh. Later, I observed the two laughing heartily about the incident.

"Dinner is served," announced Master Bates. Sgt. Lee escorted the cooks carrying the dinner to the table, and they served the food family style in bowls placed conveniently on the long table. There were mashed potatoes, fried chicken, chicken gravy, corn, green beans, corn bread, biscuits, apple cobbler, milk, tea and coffee. They set a basket of fruit at the center of the table. It contained lemons, which became my favorite citrus. Hiram and I ate hearty for it had been eight hours since our last meal. After dinner we were taken to our quarters, Jefferson Hall. It contained two large adjoining rooms with fireplaces. Each room contained eight barracks beds, desks and two bathtubs. Hand pumps delivered cold running water to the tubs and wash basins. Heating water in a fireplace kettle and adding it to the cold water made the baths warm.

The first eight were assigned to the first barracks room, and Rosecran and Custer were assigned to the second barracks with upper classmen. The quartermaster issued linen for our beds. Sherman motioned for Hiram and me to choose the beds closer to the fireplace, and Mosby joined us. Hill, Butler, Longstreet and Stuart took the remaining beds near the windows.

Hill looked at James Butler and declared, "Glad we're close to the windows in case we need fresh air."

Neither my mortal nor immortal being knew at that time that I would spend a good portion of my life carrying that little aristocrat. Only my good Presbyterian nature kept me from being uncivil to the hothead. I never dreamed I would be holding his head at his death. Had he spent a few summers working with Sam he might have developed a little more respect for people. James Butler appeared to be in the same category. He and Hill were from similar backgrounds, and Butler became Hill's support. Both were from original aristocratic Virginia families who had chosen to live in fertile rich valleys nearly two hundred years ago.

The day grew to a close, and we were tired from the travel. We made our beds and straightened the quarters in general. We made small talk then retired to our beds. I smelled Hiram's liquor when he took a drink after the lights were out. I looked over at his bed, and I could see the outline of him taking a drink from his bottle, which he conveniently placed under his mattress. I lay there wandering if Josh, my brother, had slopped the hogs tonight. He was old enough to handle the task and had seen me do it often enough. Josh was small for his age. It had taken him fifteen years to attain my twelve-year height. I thought about John Henry, my youngest brother, and Sarah and Hannah, my two sisters.

The next thing I realized we were awakened by the sergeant at arms. We were allowed ten minutes to dress for breakfast, and at breakfast we were told to report to the commissary for shoes, clothing and personal care needs. The quartermaster issued me one pair dress shoes, one pair of work shoes, three denim shirts, three trousers, one coat, underclothes and my first dress cadet uniform. The quartermaster estimated my clothes and shoe sizes. This was the most clothes and shoes I had ever owned at one time. We carried our clothes to the barracks before reporting to Monroe Hall. I took my clothes directly to the wooden locker at the foot of my bunk, and I hung the dress uniform on a rack to preserve its creases.

I returned to Monroe Hall before the other cadets. I took a front seat on the far right side facing the blackboard. The schoolroom contained fifty desks and a potbellied coal burning heating stove positioned in the room's center. The coal stove meant I wouldn't have to carry firewood. In fact, the Academy's custodian carried the coal, and he made the fires for the classrooms. It was the middle of June, and there would be no fire today. Master Bates entered the room.

"Good Morning, Tom."

"Good Morning, Master Bates."

"Have you received your clothing allotment?"

"Yes sir, I've placed them in my locker and hung up my dress uniform."

As I finished conversing with Master Bates the room begin to fill with other cadets. Initially, Robert Lee told us of academy requirements. There were so many requirements, and I managed to remember the most important ones. We must salute upper classmen and upper rank, and the promotion and demerit system was explained in detail. We were advised to stay clear of the brothels on Church St. in New York City. However, we were permitted to enter Ben Havens Tavern near the city. Later I learned Ben Havens Tavern was a social place where young people congregated in the west part of the city. We were advised to always wear our denim shirts and trousers for daily wear and to wear our dress uniforms to church and formal occasions. After the introductory talk Robert Lee escorted the cadets to the artillery and musket ranges. The ranges contained two six-pound Swedish cannons and various types of musketry. We began drilling after the brief introduction to the muskets and cannons. Sgt. Lee taught us to salute, make formation and marching, and we did a lot of marching.

We returned to the barracks to prepare for dinner. Dinners were always well prepared; however, I missed Maw's cooking and dinner with the family. After dinner we were introduced to the recreation center for activities. The center had lifting weights, parallel bars, pommel horses, billiard tables and checkerboards. The favorite activity took place on the four billiards tables, and everyone played billiards except me. Some lifted weights, and very few approached the parallel bars and pommel horse. The bars and horses required great coordination and dexterity. We returned to the barracks after the evening activities to become better acquainted. As we sat on the barracks' porch Hiram inquired about Clarksburg.

"Tom, tell us about Clarksburg, and what people do to earn a living."

"Well Hiram, it's a small place in the mountains. The major industries are farming and coal mining. Tell me about Cincinnati. I hear it's a big city on the Ohio River."

"It is, Tom. However, we only live in Cincinnati. Our tannery business is in Covington. We get a higher quality of labor from the Kentucky farm boys. They don't mind getting their hands dirty."

Hill and Butler arrived at the barracks cutting our conversations short. Butler asked.

"Tom, what do you think of the Academy?"

And before I could answer Hill looked in my direction and said.

"I bet a down creek Virginia boy from Clarksburg has never seen anything like this before."

He was right, and I hadn't been out of Clarksburg until now, and I was adapting fast to my surroundings. Before I could say anything Mosby spoke.

"Hey A.P., according to my geography Clarksburg is up in the mountains making Tom an up creek Virginia boy, and the last time I noticed water flows from the mountains to the lowlands below." Both Hill and Butler entered the barracks without tarrying longer on the porch. From that time on I always liked Mosby.

Hiram, Longstreet, Sherman and I proceeded inside the barracks. Hill and Butler had already gone to bed. We went to bed and again I observed Hiram taking the bottle from under his mattress. I could smell the liquor as he took a little snort. After he finished he returned the bottle to its hiding place. The next day began with breakfast followed by the assignment of our daily tasks. Our first assignment was the horse we would ride and care for. Each horse had an assigned stall, and part of our daily tasks was to keep the stall clean. All horses were assigned except one large stallion, Big George. No cadet in the academy's history had ever ridden Big George. He was a hand and a half larger than any other horse. During the horse assignments Hiram made a request.

"Master Duncan, may I be assigned Big George?"

"Sure Hiram. If you can ride and manage him he's yours."

"I have some horse riding experience on the farm back in Cincinnati."

"If you find he's too much horse for you, I'll allow you to choose another one."

My mare was Little Sorrell, and we became great friends. Cadets were assigned to curry the horses, soap the saddles and clean the stalls. We were allowed time with the horses before lunch, and this gave me time to saddle and ride Little Sorrell.

After lunch we registered for classes in Monroe Hall. I registered for natural philosophy, mathematics, literature, riding, musketry and artillery. Most cadets avoided natural philosophy because it required more studying to learn the mechanical applications. There were only ten cadets in the natural philosophy class. Its contents helped me greatly with my artillery class and applications in the Mexican War. When class registration was over we gathered on the musket range for drills. We practiced formations, marching and saluting again. We marched so much that I began thinking the Academy training was all about marching. When the marching was completed we were instructed to officially begin formal saluting on the following Monday. Demerits would be issued for failure to salute. We retired to the barracks to prepare for dinner. After dinner Robert Lee escorted us to a nearby stream we could use for fishing and swimming. Later, I found this stream to be a place for study and solitude. The stream was about thirty yards wide, and it had many shallow areas for wading. At bedtime I counted my money again, and I still had the dollar and seventy-five cents. I noted Hiram again doing his usual ritual after lights were out. As I lay there in bed my thoughts returned home and to Elinor.

I awoke before the sergeant of arms performed his morning task of waking everyone. We had breakfast and the quartermaster announced we would receive our first pay for the month. He issued everyone eighteen dollars, and I was glad for Hiram would not need to borrow more money from me. This gave me a total of nineteen dollars and seventy-five cents, the most money I had ever had at one time. The remainder of Friday was spent marching, making formations and saluting. We were beginning to learn the Academy's routines. It had been a stressful day, and we turned in early that night.

Again I was awake before the sergeant of arms performed his ritual. Saturday after breakfast we were given haircuts and taken to the marching area. After two hours of marching we were given the remainder of the day off. Formal dress was required for church services Sunday, and the remainder of the day was for leisure, horseback riding and activities. We had to report to Monroe Hall Monday morning after breakfast for classes. We could enjoy Saturday evening in town away from the academy; however, bed check was 11:00 P.M.

McClellan, a second year cadet, informed us about Benny Havens Tavern. It was his hangout every Saturday night the preceding year. The Tavern was the local hangout for cadets, new immigrants and the local people. McClellan told stories about dancing, girls, fighting and beer drinking, and he enjoyed each in turn. J. D. McClellan was a Pennsylvania golden boy from Pittsburgh, and A. P. and James fell under his magical spell for the stories. Hiram paid close attention when he mentioned the beer drinking. Later that evening, McClellan led the group to Ben Havens Tavern with everyone dressed in their daily clothes. The experienced McClellan wore regular street clothes, which he kept in his locker for such occasion. Everyone eagerly followed McClellan for an evening of fun.

I settled in with pencil and paper to write home to the family. I told them all about West Point and the river nearby. The food was good, and I was living with seven other cadets and named them. I gave all the information I knew about each cadet, and I told them how well I got along with Robert Lee, Hiram, Mosby and Sherman. I didn't mention Hiram's lights out ritual at bedtime nor did I mention my relationship with Hill and Butler. After I finished the correspondence to the family I composed a letter to Elinor. I wrote Elinor all about the academy, and I told her about my new horse, clothes and activities. I also told her I would like to see her when I came home at Christmas furlough. After finishing the compositions I placed them in my locker to mail the next week. It was lonely in the barracks by myself so I prepared my bed and turned in. It seemed as if I had barely asleep when everyone returned from the evening at Benny Havens Tavern. Mosby and Longstreet helped Hiram to his bed. I was completely awake now so I got out of bed while McClellan led the group to seats around the table in front of the fireplace.

"Tom, you should have been with us tonight. Hill and Butler danced all night with many Irish girls. These girls were new immigrants, and they had been without male companionship for weeks on the trip from Ireland. You could have even picked a girl tonight."

"Maybe next Saturday night I go with you. I got very lonely in the barracks by myself."

Mosby removed Hiram's shoes and shirt and put him to bed. Just as he finished the sergeant of arms came in for bed check.

"Glad to see you boys made it back on time. I don't like to give demerits. Don't forget formal dress for church tomorrow."

We were up early Sunday morning getting ready for breakfast. Hiram wasn't feeling too well from the night before. He felt the after effects of having too much beer. We had breakfast and returned to the barracks to dress for church. It really felt good dressing in my new dress uniform and cap. I felt special and equal to the other cadets. A Calvinist Presbyterian minister presented church services. He spoke on the evils of drinking, and I was hoping Hiram was paying attention. We were treated to a Sunday turkey dinner. It was prepared very similar to Maw's turkey dinners with stuffing and giblet gravy. We removed our dress uniforms and put on our daily clothes to leisurely enjoy the Sunday afternoon free time. Sherman and I went down to the stream to investigate the wildlife. We saw many minnows, frogs, salamanders, muskrats and a variety of birds, and Sherman skipped rocks across the stream.

On returning from the stream I visited Little Sorrel in the stables. I curried her, cropped her mane, and I practiced putting the blanket and saddle on her. I cleaned her stable and before returning to the barracks. The barracks were lonely on Sunday afternoons even with everyone around. I missed home and Elinor. I thought about working on the farm, and I even missed slopping the hogs. We went to evening mess and gathered on the barracks porch afterwards. Hill began telling of his exploits on the dance floor at Benny Havens Tavern.

"Tom, you should have seen James and me dancing at Ben Havens Tavern. We danced to Irish fiddle jigs all night. I had a girl with long brown hair and a soft body, and James had a tall one with red hair. Now, McClellan was with three girls, whom he took turns hugging and dancing with. We could all take lessons from him. Maybe you'll go with us next week, and one of those girls may teach you to dance."

Hill's conversation was beginning to interest me. I was interested in learning everything I could, and I didn't know how to dance. I had decided to go with them next Saturday. I could always hang with Sherman, Mosby, Longstreet and maybe Hiram. We turned in, and Monday morning came soon enough. We had breakfast and went to classes in Monroe Hall.

My first class was literature followed by mathematics then Natural Philosophy. After those classes I had riding, artillery-musketry and drills. Marching was a good portion of the drills the first year. The first day we were issued books and assignments. Master Bates taught Natural Philosophy and artillery. Master Duncan taught literature and musketry. Master Johnson taught mathematics and riding. I was amazed at the books. I was issued more books than existed in Clarksburg, and I even had separate books for artillery, riding and musketry. These were practical books explaining the types, use and cleaning of the guns. The riding book explained riding and care of the horse. I didn't need a book to take care of Samantha when I was home on the farm. Before lunch I took my books to the barracks and fixed up a desk nearest the fireplace. I looked at the literature assignment and determined the reading was quite complicated for me. The mathematics was also difficult, and it started square root. Master O'Nagle had not taught square root in Clarksburg. I had only studied addition, subtraction, multiplication and long division. I was really hoping Master Bates would have good explanation of Natural Philosophy. The first class was on forces and Newton's laws of motion.

I was the first to show up for the artillery class. There were two types of cannons on the artillery range. The large cannon was a Parrott gun named for its inventor, Robert Parker Parrott. It was a muzzle-loading, rifled cannon made of cast iron. It had great accuracy at long distances, and the smaller cannon was a howitzer. It had a short barrel, and it fired multiple minie balls in a high trajectory. Master Bates introduced us to cannon history, types and parts the first day. Master Duncan started the musketry class by issuing each a Model 1816 U. S. Flintlock Musket. The musket shot a .50 caliber minie ball, which Harpers Ferry Armory and Springfield Armory manufactured. My musket contained a bayonet lug. We were taught complete assembly and maintenance for the musket. Some cadets gave their musket a feminine name.

I proportioned my time to spend most of it on the more difficult courses. I read my literature assignment first. There were many words I had to look up in the glossary. Then I reviewed my math assignment, square roots. It appeared to be a combination of multiplying and dividing, and I was struggling with the concept when Mosby came by.

"What the problem, Tom?"

"John, the concept of square roots is not exactly straight forward compared to multiplying and dividing."

"It's as easy as two times two, Tom. The square root of four is plus or minus two. To check you answer you multiply two times two equals four and minus two times minus two equals four."

"That seems simple enough, John. But when you multiply two times minus two you get minus four not the original four you square rooted."

"True, Tom. This is one of the major rules of square root. You must always multiply numbers with like signs to produce the original number. When you square root a number the answer is always a plus or minus number and not a plus and minus number."

After working a few problems with Mosby I was beginning to get the hang of square root. Boy, did I feel good. I could square root the plus or minus kind.

"Thanks, Mosby."

"Hang with it Tom. You'll do alright."

Thanks to Mosby I would have more time for Natural Philosophy, and the first chapter begin with Sir Isaac Newton's Laws. I read the chapter and committed Newton's three laws of motion to memory. The first one was a body remains at rest until a force act upon it, and the second one was if a force acts on a body it will accelerate in the direction of the force proportional to the force and inversely to the mass of the body. The third law was more complex. It stated that each time a force acted on a body there was an equal and opposite force from the body. Chapter one introduced me to the relationship between mass and weight. Weight is the mass of a body times the pull of gravity, 32.2 ft/square sec. If a cannon ball mass were one slug, its weight would be 32.2 pounds (1 slug x 32.2 ft/square sec.). The 32.2 ft/square seconds is the earth's gravitational pull. This was an interesting concept, and I had never seen calculations like this before. I could see where there would be many applications for this kind of calculation. Just as I was finishing my Natural Philosophy Custer entered our barracks.

"How are you doing, Hiram?"

Hiram looked at him, "I'm doing alright. What's it to you?"

"I'm just checking to see if the beer and liquor is having any affect on you."

"Did your mother have any real male children, George?"

Antagonizing Hiram, Custer asked, "Hiram, did you ever decide what your real name is? You didn't even know your name when you registered." He laughed mockingly, "My name is Hiram…Ulysess…Simpson Grant."

"That's about enough of your shit, Custer. Maybe I should take you down by the river and give you a good thrashing."

Before Custer could answer Robert Lee stepped through the door. "How's the studying going, boys? George, do you belong in this barracks?"

Custer saluted, "No, Sir. I'm in the next barracks adjoining this one. I came over for a study break."

"You'd better return there to your studying. Classes are difficult here at the academy."

"Yes Sir," Custer saluted and returned to his barracks.

"How's your studying going, Tom?" Lee inquired.

"I'm learning a lot of new concepts. We didn't have so many books in Clarksburg, and we didn't have teachers that taught concepts like these either."

Everyone saluted Lee as he turned to leave. After Lee left, Butler spoke.

"This stuff is old hat to me. I studied this in school back in Charlottesville. If it's all like this I won't have to study. How about you A. P.?"

"It's a review for me also. I wasn't planning on spending all my time here studying. We want to have fun, don't we? Meet some ladies."

It was late, and we were starting to turn in. I lay in my bed thinking of home and Elinor. I had been so busy all day that I hardly had time to think of anything other than school. I mailed the letter I wrote Saturday, and I wondered about Josh slopping the hogs. The next day repeated the first. We were reading more literature stories, and the square root concept Mosby taught me was the same one Master Johnson taught the next day. By the end of class I could square root 25, 49, 64, 81 and 100. Master Bates presented so many different unit systems for the Newton law concepts, that it was confusing. I believe if he had taught one unit system it would have been easier to learn.

We continued the week with classes, saluting and marching. The weather was hot; however, we managed to sleep. Cold baths helped us cool down before going to bed. Friday evening was an interesting occasion with a gathering in our barracks. McClellan was giving us a lecture on the importance of attending the academy.

"Men, attending the academy is now a timely opportunity. We are not going to be subjected to the same political forces as our forefathers, George Washington and Andrew Jackson. What we need once we finish here at the academy is a good war to propel us to a political career."

I noticed Custer absorbing everything he was saying, and I was beginning to believe McClellan was becoming Custer's hero.

McClellan continued, "My goals after the academy are to become a general and later president."

Custer could contain his feelings no longer, "I want to be a general and a war hero."

At that point Grant and Sherman, Longstreet, Mosby, Hill and Butler laughed. Hill changed the dialogue to another topic.

"Are we still going to Benny Havens Tavern tomorrow night, McClellan?"

"Sure. Why shouldn't we? We had a good time last week, and those three ladies are waiting my return. I noticed you and James were having a good time dancing with the ladies." He turned looking at me.

"Are you going with us, Tom?

"Maybe."

Everyone applauded.

Longstreet spoke up, "Tom, these New York immigrants may be a little different from those Virginia hill girls.

Sherman joined in, "Yea, Tom. They may have three tits."

I expected such a statement from Sherman.

Everyone laughed.

Grant spoke up, "Sherman, you're crazy." The name stuck, and the next day some of the cadets were still calling him Crazy Sherman. Later he would be accused of being crazy after expressing to the newspaper that hundreds, even thousand lives would be lost to win the war.

A.P. added his two cents worth, "Tom, we may find a girl for you. Who knows you may not be a virgin when she gets through with you. Girls with three tits may not bother you. You've been use to cows with four tits back on the farm. How did you milk those cows on the side of the hill? Did you sit on the milking stool uphill or downhill?"

Lee had overheard Hill's fun making and intervened, "You know Hill sometimes we have wrestling in our drills, and maybe you can have Tom as an opponent. I think it's time we turned in for some sleep." We saluted and he bid us goodnight.

Saturday morning came, and we had our drills, rode the horses and cleaned the stalls. I used the afternoon to study down by the river. It was a great place to read literature, and I always read more in my literature book than my assignment. Saturday evening finally came and everyone had a bath. Anticipation grew among the group thinking of the evening. McClellan wore his store bought clothes again. We passed the O'Malley farm on the way to Ben Havens Tavern. The farm adjoined the academy on the eastside. It was mainly a vegetable farm with horses, hogs, chickens, goats and other miscellaneous animals much like our farm in Clarksburg.

I investigated the Ben Havens Tavern establishment, and there found two billiards tables and a card playing room. Hiram and Sherman were really interested in the card playing room, and I watched McClellan, Hill, Butler and Longstreet play billiards. It didn't appear to be that difficult to play and I thought I would play if given the chance. I had not played billiards in the Academy's recreation center yet. Sure enough a table became available and Mosby and I played.

"Have you ever played this game before, Tom?"

"No, John. I never had time to get to town much. I always had to work the farm."

"Well, that's alright. I taught you square root, and now I'll teach you billiards. You shoot the white cue ball with the pool stick into the numbered balls. The objective is to put the numbered balls into the six billiard table pockets, and the one making the most balls wins."

Mosby shot first, and he didn't make anything so it was my shot. My shot only moved some balls around on the table. John shot again making two balls with one shot. He shot again and didn't make anything. I shot and made one ball, and it was becoming more fun. I shot again but was so excited from making my first shot that I didn't make anything. We heard the fiddle music begin in the large room containing the bar so we hurriedly finished the game and joined everyone.

The young ladies from the city trickled into Benny Havens Tavern until all the tables were filled. Next, the bar and standing room were filled with cadets and young ladies, and the fiddling had everyone in a dancing mood. Everyone danced jigs and waltzes. McClellan, Hill and Butler were having a good time dancing with the young ladies. Longstreet wandered through the dancers approaching John.

"Have you seen Hiram and Sherm?"

Mosby answered, "They disappeared into the card room."

"Try to keep an eye on them, Tom"

"Okay." I replied.

John and Longstreet left the bar to join the dancing. As they left, a raven-haired young lady occupied the vacant seat next to me.

"Howdy, cadet. What your name?"

"I'm Tom Jackson. What's yours?"

"Mary Morrison from Kerry, Ireland. Where are you from?"

"Clarksburg, Virginia."

"Well, Tom Jackson from Clarksburg, let's dance." She grabbed my hand, and we joined everyone on the floor. I had never danced before. She hooked her left arm into my left arm and danced to the left. Then she turned hooking her right arm into my right arm and danced in the opposite direction. I followed until the fiddling stopped, and we took our seats at the bar.

"Tom, have you ever danced before?"

"No."

"I must make it a chore to teach you. You follow me and keep time to the music."

"What's keeping time?"

"Never mind. Just follow me."

We danced tune after tune until Hiram and Sherm came to the bar. Sherm had won thirty-two dollars, and Hiram was inebriated and broke. Hiram looked at Mary and me.

"Tom, who's the girl?"

"Mary Morrison. She's teaching me to dance."

"Loan me enough to buy a drink. I lost this month's pay in the card game."

Sherm interrupted, "I'll buy you one, Hiram. After all I won most of the money." Sherman bought the next two rounds for Hiram. Then it was time to return to the barracks, and Hiram could hardly walk. He borrowed money from Sherm to buy a bottle for the road. I told Mary goodnight and thanked her for teaching me to dance. We agreed to meet there again next Saturday.

Sherm, Mosby, Longstreet and I helped Hiram all the way to the barracks. After reaching the barracks we put Grant to bed just before bed check. We turned in, and I lay there reminiscing about the evening. I couldn't believe a girl taught me to dance, and she was really nice. I squeezed her the same as McClellan squeezed the girls he was dancing with, and she liked it. I tried to sleep, and the academy's mascot, Sarge, made noise all during the night and kept us awake. He needed to answer the nature call and become exposed to animal husbandry. His baying produced many complaints Sunday morning. Butler complained first.

"Did you hear the noise Sarge was making last night?"

"He's in need," Longstreet explained.

Hill intercedes, "Let's give him some saltpeter."

It was apparent these cadets didn't understand farm animals.

"We'll take him to O'Malley's farm. I noticed the farmer has three nannies, in the meantime we'll have to bear the noise at night."

Sure enough Sarge bayed every night all week, and he drove us crazy. It was a short trip for Sherm for he was already crazy.

Sunday morning came too soon. We dressed, and went to church and dinner. The afternoon was free, and I went to the river with my mathematics book. We were still studying square root; however, square rooting was getting more difficult. I could square root 4, 9, 16, 25, 36, 49, 64, 81 and 100 without any difficulty. Now, we studied the square rooting large numbers. It was like division with a different mathematical method applied. The book wasn't too clear on the explanation for performing the task. After much deliberation trying to understand the rules and example, I decided to return to the barracks and study Natural Philosophy. Mosby was completing his studies when I arrived at the barracks.

"John", I said, "You taught me to square root, and now it's getting more difficult. It's a combination of division and multiplication, and I can't figure it out anymore."

"Ah pshaw, Tom. Let's have a look at it."

John studied the assignment.

"Tom, this is going to take me about five minutes to demonstrate the mathematical technique."

"Thanks, John."

"Let's start with an easy example. Let's square root six hundred twenty-five. We already know the answer is plus or minus twenty-five. To demonstrate the technique, write six hundred twenty-five under the square root sign. Now divide the numbers in sets of two or less which make the only division between the six and two. What number squared is equal to or less than six, the first number set under the square root sign?"

"That's two"

"Right. First write the number two on top of the square root sign over the six, and double the two to make four and multiply it by ten to produce the number forty. Also write the number four under the six, and subtract the four from six leaving two. Now bring down the other set under the square root sign placing the set next to the two making the number two hundred twenty-five. Divide the number forty into the two hundred twenty-five. It divides five times, and now you add the five to the forty. Also place the five over the square root sign above the second set of numbers. Multiply the forty-five by five to produce the number two hundred twenty-five. Subtract two hundred twenty-five from two hundred twenty-five. The subtraction answer is zero, and the problem is solved. The answer is plus or minus twenty-five, and to check your answer you multiply twenty-five by twenty-five."

"Thank you, John Singleton".

With my newly found knowledge I was off to the river again, and I worked homework problems the rest of the day. I worked the next assignment in the book, and I realized that I learned something new. After finishing the problems I sat by the river, and I thought about last night, Mary, Elinor, Maw, Paw, John Henry, Sarah, Hannah, and Josh slopping the hogs. Later I stopped by the barn and curried Little Sorrell. I went to supper, then back to the barracks for more studying.

The Natural Philosophy homework problem was an energy related problem having to solve the force required to shoot a twelve pound cannon ball through a four foot cannon with a velocity of two hundred feet per second. This was a work-energy problem, and work produced equals the kinetic energy gained by the cannon ball. The given formula was force times cannon length equals one-half cannon ball mass times cannon ball velocity. Solving for the force required squaring the velocity, 200 ft/sec, times the ball weight, 12 pounds, divided by thirty-two slugs and dividing by eight. The resolved force calculated at 1875 pounds. The book contained a similar example that enabled me to solve the problem. This problem type was interesting for it appeared to have a practical application. I continued to read my Natural Philosophy after working the home-work problem, and again I was thankful for having books to read, opportunity for an education and being able to make friends.

Everyone settled into the Academy's regiments, and the evenings were spent quietly studying. We were in bed prior to bed check, and again I smelled Grant's nightly libations. I was growing used to it, and I would have thought him sick had I not smelled his whiskey. Grant always studied his subjects, and he was always prepared for exams. He was an average student, but he could have made higher marks with a little more effort.

Again my thoughts turned to Mary, Elinor and home. Sarge's nightly recitals woke everyone from initial sleep, and Longstreet was the first to speak up.

"Tom, when are we going to do something about Sarge?"

"Go to sleep", said Butler. "We'll let Tom work out this problem."

Sherman spoke, "I'll help you, Tom. How about you A.P.?"

"I'm in. We'll take it on as a barracks task."

Sarge settled down and the next thing we heard was the wake up call.

Classes had become more interesting now. Artillery and musketry had become fun. We assembled-disassembled muskets and cannons until we could do it with our eyes closed. We also practiced the operation with our side arm. Tomorrow, we begin firing the cannons and muskets without load. Master Duncan and Bates told us the exercise would introduce us to the smell of the gases produced by the gunpowder. They were right. The smell of nitrogen dioxide, sulfur dioxide and carbon dioxide was overwhelming. The sulfur dioxide became absorbed in our clothes, and it made the entire barracks smell like sulfur. We grew used to it for it was becoming more of what I expected the Academy to be like. I expected to be educated and taught the art of war defense.

Thursday rolled around, and I received two letters. Elinor sent one, and Maw sent the other. Elinor had received my letter, and she wrote to tell me the good fortune of her family. Albert, her Paw, had borrowed money, and he had bought a mercantile business in Clarksburg. She and the boys operated the business. She missed seeing me at church, and she looked forward to the Christmas break. Maw said Josh was adapting to slopping the hogs, but he didn't like the task. Paw was still operating the farm and mill, and he often remarked that he missed my help.

The classes were tolerated so we could get on with military learning, and I really took interest in the cannons. We charged the cannons with powder and shot blanks repeatedly, and at the end of the artillery and musket classes we cleaned the guns. We continued the fun riding and horsemanship classes. We also curried the horses and clean the stables, and we developed riding competition. My mare was disadvantaged in height and carrying my weight; however, we participated even though everyone beat us. Hiram was the leader. He rode Big George, the fastest horse. He was quite a horseman, and he won all the races.

The week flew by fast, and it was time to put our Friday plan in place to take care of Sarge's desires. Our barracks' cadets gathered at the central table for assignments. After dark I was to rope Sarge with the aid of Hiram and Sherm, and it was my job to lead him to O'Malley's farm. Butler, Hill, Longstreet and Mosby were up front leading the way, and Stuart and Rosecran were to serve as lookouts. The plan was in place, and we waited. Sarge started baying just after dark. We approached him in the pasture, and I placed the rope around his neck. Hiram and Sherm each grabbed a horn, and the tussle began. I pulled hard on the rope, and he began to follow. I pulled Sarge, while my companions ran along the road toward O'Malley's farm. Mosby and Longstreet had the gate open when we arrived, and I led Sarge inside the pasture. We hurriedly removed the rope and set Sarge free. Then we assumed a watch outside the pasture while Sarge performed his duty.

After two hours Sarge and the nannies were satisfied. Hill and Butler crossed into the pasture to retrieve Sarge and he attacked them with his head lowered. They escaped by jumping the fence, and we developed another plan to get Sarge back to the Academy. Everyone entered the pasture simultaneously in the attempt to capture Sarge. Sarge chased everyone in turn. Finally, Sarge tired and I put the rope around his neck. Stuart and Sherm grabbed the horns, and everyone began helping. I was beginning to think Sarge didn't want to leave. We pulled Sarge back to the Academy and placed him safely in his stall.

"Good evening, boys", said Robert.

"Attention!" we all saluted.

"I see you boys performed the annual ceremony to relieve Sarge's natural pressure. Our mascot usually has these same symptoms about this time every year. O'Malley doesn't mind the prank, and he usually benefits from the offsprings. Sarge has sired all his nannies, and there exist many tales of these escapades. Demerits are given if you're caught doing this prank, and you know I've never had a demerit. I was never caught. Cadets, this is your first lesson in becoming a gentleman, and thanks for quieting Sarge. Maybe we can all get a little sleep now. Be sure to close the stall door. Good night."

We headed for the barracks, and once inside we began to laugh and celebrate. We were even glad that Hill and Butler had survived being chased by Sarge. We laughed and A.P. and James joined our laughter. We would relive that night over and over, and Butler and Hill became friendlier toward me. However, I always knew I was the down creek Virginia boy to them. This was one night I would not be writing home to Paw about, and maybe I could share this moment with him when I returned home. He would be proud of me, and it was something he would have done. We turned in to prepare for Saturday's drills and Benny Havens Tavern on Saturday night. We had a good nights sleep.

Saturday evening, we prepared to go to Benny Havens Tavern; however, it was difficult to find sulfur-free smelling clothes. Even McClellan's store clothes contained the sulfur smell. His store clothes picked up the sulfur smell from being stored with his daily cadet clothes. We arrived late to Ben Havens Tavern, and the ladies were waiting except for Mary Morrison. There were three for McClellan and one each for Hill and Butler. The remaining cadets entered the billiards parlor and began shooting billiards. The fiddler began to fiddle, and we entered the bar and dancing area. We sat at the bar with Hiram seated next to me.

"Tom, loan me a dollar until I get paid."

I had forgotten Hiram had lost all his pay the last time we were here. "Okay, Hiram. You must remember to repay me at payday."

"Thanks, Tom."

I bought us both beers, and we toasted the night.

Suddenly, a familiar female voice appeared next to me, "Hello, Mr. West Point."

It was Mary, and that made my evening. We drank and danced all night. She taught me a new dance, the waltz. It was a slower dance stepping in a box step. The fiddle music played less lively for waltzes compared to an Irish jig. Again we danced all evening, I squeezed her hand, and she squeezed mine. I hugged her and she hugged me, and we went to the bar in time for Hiram to borrow another dollar. A little earlier I noted McClellan, Hill and Butler had slipped outside with their ladies. Ben Havens Tavern was surrounded with flat land and trees, which made it nice for an evening stroll. It wasn't difficult to ascertain where they had disappeared, and I would hear about it later.

Hiram had almost passed out at the bar. He had consumed the two dollars worth of liquor. Mosby, Sherm and Longstreet came to the bar in time to help me get Hiram back to the barracks. Shortly after we got to the barracks McClellan, Hill and Butler came in, and Hill looked my way.

"Tom, you old dog, you were really dancing with Miss Mary tonight. You should have been with us. We were doing some different kind of squeezing of our own. McClellan was kissing all three of his ladies. He's really a weird guy."

Butler said, "I didn't notice. I was too busy kissing my own."

A.P. laughed, "We mustn't tell. We must remember we're the Academy's gentlemen cadets. Even Robert E. said so."

We put Hiram to bed just as he past out. We continued to reminisce about the evening when bed check was performed. All except Hiram received a demerit for not being ready for bed.

It was Sunday, and Hiram was feeling better. He missed breakfast, but he went to church. After dinner we deposited our sulfur smelling clothes at the laundry. The afternoon was utilized studying and preparing for classes. On Monday, we were to use live ammunition in the cannons and flintlocks. Masters Bates and Duncan demonstrated the loading techniques, and after loading the Parrot cannon we fired a twelve-pound ball into a field about five hundred yards away. Master Bates demonstrated this artillery firing ten more times. Then he addressed the class asking for volunteers to fire the cannon, and I immediately volunteered. Loading the cannons and moving them about was all physical work just as I had performed on the farm. The cannon was hot so I had to be careful in loading the ball, and I applied extra care loading the charge. I inserted the fuse and set it off, and the cannon fired in the same area of the field where Master Bates had shot earlier. Master Bates looked at me.

"Very good! You'll make a good cannon officer. Do it again."

I reloaded and shot in the same area again.

"Now Tom, cut the charge in half and fire again."

I did as ordered. The twelve-pound ball only went a third of the distance as my first shot.

"What did you learn from that shot compared to the first shot?"

"Cutting the charge in half does not mean you cut the distance in half."

"That's correct, Tom. When you cut the charge in half you have half the amount of energy forcing the ball through the cannon. However, it's not just a weight, energy and friction function. It's a weight, energy, friction and volume function. You have twice the energy expended in a fixed volume forcing the cannon ball out the nozzle when a full charge is ignited."

I tried to correlate this explanation to the Natural Philosophy problem of muzzle velocity I had studied earlier; however, there seemed to be no correlation. It was an exciting time, and everyone took turns firing the cannon. I fired it two more times before the class ended. In Master Duncan's class we loaded our own muskets and fired them into targets. We had to learn the variance for our gun to hit the target dead center, and we improved with each shot. At day's end our ears were ringing from the shooting noise. Mathematics and Natural Philosophy classes became discussions for artillery and musketry. Everyone bragged about respective capabilities, and Custer was the most outspoken. I would not have wanted to live off the hunting game he might have provided from his musket skills. We would have starved. I squirrel hunted with a musket back home on the farm, and it was nothing new for me to shoot the musket. My enjoyment came from the cannon. I could hardly wait to fire the Howitzer cannon. We grew use to Custer's bragging in the barracks. Per George, he could run faster, shoot straighter and was better looking than anyone else.

We were getting less homework now, allowing more time for the horses. Little Sorrell had become my favorite friend. I curried her and fed her an apple from the evening mess. I had taken an orange and apple for an evening snack. I would have had a lemon, but I had exhausted the lemon supply two days earlier. I developed quite an appetite for citrus fruit. Eating oranges, grapefruit and lemons was a new taste experience for me, and lemons were my favorite. They were sourer than unripe apples, and I would feel physically better when I ate citrus. Citrus was good for my blood circulation.

The next day we spent artillery and musket classes disassembling and cleaning the cannon and muskets. One day we shot the guns, and the next we cleaned and reassembled the guns. I would learn later that I had gained much wisdom in performing these tasks. During the war many techniques were used to keep the cannons and muskets firing. Cannon maintenance was performed in the field under warring conditions. Weeks were becoming like days, and everyday was filled with studying and activities. I had written two more letters home. I wrote a letter to Elinor and one to the family. I hardly thought about Elinor anymore. My fantasies were occupied for spending time with Mary at Ben Havens Tavern.

This week we were taught how to shoot the Howitzer. Its load was five quarter pound balls chained together. It had a short elevated barrel, and the load was shot at elevation for short distances. It was designed to repel the oncoming enemy charges, and like the Parrot, its construction was cast iron. A lighter metal construction would have made it a more efficient weapon. It required three to four men to move these weapons. Once the cannon was used, the cannon barrels became hot, and touching the barrels could produce severe burns. Sometimes horses pulled the cannons from one position to another for more firing efficiency.

It was September, and we were making coal fires in the two fireplaces. We took turns filling the coal buckets from the Academy's coal bin, and we banked the fires every night so we didn't have to rebuild the fires each morning. I always added extra coal to the fire to provide light for more time to study Mathematics and Natural Philosophy. I had originally picked a desk closer to the fireplace for these occasions. These continuous fires made it more convenient to heat bath water for the Saturday night at Benny Havens.

We had been paid again, and Hiram returned the two dollars he borrowed. He didn't remember the second dollar, and I finally convinced him that he had borrowed it. I told him it was simple. If he didn't repay me he should not ask to borrow more money. I didn't mention the breakfast I had bought him on the train. He didn't mention it, and I just considered it an act of charity. He never had the ability to deal in money matters throughout his life. It was Friday night just before bedtime, and I turned to Hiram.

"Do you want me to take care of some of your money when we go to Ben Havens Tavern tomorrow night?"

"I can look after my own money."

"I was just offering to help you out."

"Thanks. I'll be alright."

When we went to bed my thoughts turned to tomorrow night at Ben Havens. I thought about it with anticipation hoping to see Mary there again. We did the Saturday morning and afternoon exercises. Finally, we prepared for our Saturday night amusement at Ben Havens Tavern. I was disappointed not to find Mary Morrison there. I played billiards and listened to the fiddle music, but the music had no meaning without Mary. I joined Hiram and Sherm at the bar, and I drank my first beer with these friends. It tasted good and made me feel uncontrollable. After I finished the beer, I approached a girl wearing a white dress with brown hair.

"Let's dance." I expected her to answer in the affirmative since there were more girls there than cadets.

She acted surprised, "Why, of course."

We moved to the floor and danced, and I was feeling good. I was dancing after the music stopped, and she was embarrassed. She didn't dance with me anymore, and it was her loss. Had she only known I was to become a great general, and she was given opportunity. I was going to have another beer but Mosby dissuaded me. It was time to return to the barracks. On the way to the Academy, Longstreet and Mosby were accompanying me, and they struck up a catchy tune. After the first stanza we all sang together.

"Roll me over in the clover, Roll me over in the clover, Roll me over lay me down and…."

At that point they burst into laughter, and so did I. It was a happy evening, and we didn't even get any demerits. Just before turning in Jeb addressed everyone.

"Boys, you know Old Tom is getting to be just like the rest of us. He enjoys having a good time same as we do."

"Amen!" I replied. Then I went to sleep with my clothes on.

I spent Sunday recovering from Saturday night. I went to church and after-wards to dinner. As the day wore on I gained enough energy to go to the river and visit the stable. On Monday night thirty minutes after bed check, I noticed Hill and Butler slipping out of the barracks through a window. Before daybreak the next morning they returned. I overheard them talking the next day. They had arranged to meet their girlfriends.

Vicente Guerrero, Emperor of Mexico, expansionistic ideals occupied the Academy's topic for discussion much as it did the national leaders. Guerrero upset the president to the point of initiating his overthrow. Finally, the senate elected to overthrow Guerrero by supporting a group led by Antonio Lopez de Santa Anna. Santa Anna was a supporter of Guerrero until he became aggressive in his national policies, and at that time Santa Anna sought the support of the United States. The president brought Santa Anna to Washington for training, and he remained in Washington for six months before returning to Mexico. He began organizing Mexico's peasants to overthrow Guerrero, and after a two-year campaign he successfully overthrew Guerrero to become dictator of Mexico. His first initiative was to rebuild the Mexican army. He employed all strategies learned in Washington, and he had learned his lessons well.

West Point leadership was always interested in national and international endeavors. Academy leaders realized Winfield Scott and many other United States generals were growing older, and they would depend on younger Academy officers. We would eventually grow into leadership positions in this army. I con-tinued to read and study even though my marks were only marginal. Lee contin-ued to give me encouragement, and Artillery, Musketry and Natural Philosophy were my favorite classes. I continued to ride and curry Little Sorrell at every opportunity. Each night before going to sleep I thought about not seeing Mary at Ben Havens Tavern, and sometimes my thoughts drifted to Elinor Junkins. However, it was Mary Morrison, the girl full of life and vigor that occupied my fantasies. She danced and teased the evening away, and it was better dancing with her than drinking all the beer at Benny Havens Tavern. It was fun doing all the new things with the cadets.

The next evening was chilly for September, and as we entered the barracks we noticed the fires were out in the fireplaces. Hill looked at Hiram.

"Who carried the coal last night and was responsible for banking the fires?"

Hiram returned his gaze, "I carried the coal and I banked the fireplaces. All the coal burned, and the fire went out."

"No excuse, Hiram. You must rebuild the fires."

"That's no problem. I'll rebuild the fires with the remainder of the coal I carried last night. Isn't it your turn to bring in the coal?"

"Don't worry about me. I carry my portion of coal, and I bank a fire so it won't go out."

That wasn't the last time two or three cadets would have that discussion. The fires would go out many times during the winter. Sometimes I would bring in the coal and build the fires even when it wasn't my turn. I had learned the fire-building lesson well at school in Clarksburg. During the next two months I received letters from Elinor and the family. Classes were really getting harder, and I had missed going to Ben Havens Tavern at least three times. When I did go it was to play billiards, listen to music and drink beer. I had not danced anymore since the night I drank the first beer. Once passing O'Malley's farm on the way to Ben Havens Tavern I noticed the three nannies were pregnant, and I thought before too long we may have three little Sarges running around the farm nursing.

It was early November and Saturday, and I was tired of studying. I was determined to go to Benny Havens Tavern. I prepared like everyone else, and prior to leaving everyone celebrated that I was taking a study break. We arrived early and I had a beer, and Hiram and I played billiards. Of course, I paid for the billiards. Jeb, Rosecran and Sherm went to the poker room while Hiram, Mosby and I found a table near the fiddler and ordered three beers. The dancing started and Mosby found a partner to dance a jig while Hiram and I watched. The next jig Hiram found a partner and danced. I didn't know he could dance. I identified a blond-headed girl across the dance floor, and I decided the next dance I would dance with her. The next dance was a waltz, and we danced. I remembered the waltz moves Mary had taught me. This wasn't Mary, but it was fun dancing with her. I learned her name was Millie Johnson. We danced all evening, and we agreed to meet again next Saturday night. Hiram didn't require help going to the barracks, and as we passed O'Malley's farm he brayed like a goat. The goats returned his bray.

We celebrated Thanksgiving in the barracks and at mess. We went to Ben Havens Tavern the last Saturday before December furlough. I was dancing with Millie when she noticed Hill and Butler going outside with their ladies, and she recommended we join them. I agreed to go outside, but I didn't want to accompany A.P. and James with their girls. We walked to the back of Ben Havens Tavern, and she pulled me toward the trees. It appeared to be a good idea so I followed, and just as we were in the trees she gave me a kiss on the lips. I quickly mastered the art of kissing, and in fact, I couldn't get enough kissing. Millie was a good kisser, and we stay there for about a half-hour kissing. She pulled away.

"Tom, we must return to the dance. I'm thirsty, and I want to dance some more."

"Okay." I remarked. I didn't understand, and she was enjoying the activity so much. I was disappointed, and I didn't understand why she wanted to quit. My immortal state has given me greater understanding of that distinct incident. Once inside we danced to waltzes, and she snuggled close. The evening was over, and we were in the barracks with everyone celebrating. There was no bed check that night for the next morning we would begin our trip home. The Academy had already furnished us with train tickets. A.P. was making plans with Butler to return to the Academy two days early to see New York City.

"James, I'll come to your house in Charlottesville three days before we have to return. I'll spend the night, and we'll travel to New York City for rest and relaxation before returning here."

"Sounds like a plan to me, Ambrose."

It was the first time I had heard Hill's first name, Ambrose, and he was giving me a hard time. Ambrose! No wander he had everyone calling him Hill or A.P. It wouldn't surprise me to find out the P stood for Prissy.

Early the next morning Hiram and I caught the train to Pittsburgh. There we split with me going on to Clarksburg. I spent six hours in the station at Pittsburgh before the next train. The family had turned out to greet me at the station. Josh was the first to greet me, followed by Paw and my other brother and sisters. I finally made it to Maw, and she gave me a hug.

"Son, what's that smell in your clothes? It smells like sulfur."

"It's gunpowder from artillery and musket practice. We use a lot of gunpowder everyday."

Paw cut in saying, "Josh, you get Tom's bag. Let's get him on home, then he can tell us about West Point."

Josh threw my bag on the wagon, and the family loaded up for home. Everyone was very anxious to hear about the Academy. John Henry wanted to know if there were girls at West Point. We finally arrived at home, and Paw added wood to the fireplace. The women went to the kitchen to prepare dinner. I was allowed time to wash, refresh and unpack, and Josh and John followed me from room to room asking questions. Just as I finished unpacking a yell came from the kitchen.

"Dinner is ready!"

We gathered around the table to one of Maw's fried chicken dinners with mashed potatoes, gravy and apple pie for desert. After dinner the women cleaned the table and dishes while the rest of us retired to the fireplace. Paw and my brothers were anxious for West Point stories, and I knew not to start any stories without Maw and the girls. Finally, they joined us to learn about the Academy. I began.

"Well, I know you want to know about West Point, and there's a lot to tell that's happened the past few months. First, I met a boy named Hiram Grant on the train in Pittsburgh going to West Point. After two days of travel and a layover in Pittsburgh, we arrived at West Point. Robert Lee met us and introduced us to other cadets. Afterwards we had dinner and were given a barracks to sleep in. I chose my bed and desk near the fireplace with plans to study after going to bed. The cadets came from all over, but mostly they're from Virginia. One boy from the Virginia valleys called me a down creek Virginia boy. I'm learning Mathematics, Literature, Natural Philosophy, artillery and musketry. My favorite class is artillery. We have two cannons, and I can fire both of them. We are taught marching and saluting, and we ride horses and clean stables. I have my own mare named Little Sorrell. In the Academy mess hall we eat oranges, lemons and sometimes grapefruit in addition to the regular food they prepare for us." At that point John asked me.

"Tom, what's a grapefruit?"

"It's citrus. It's grown in a warmer climate. All citrus have thick skins, and they are usually sour. It's like eating a green apple, only sourer."

"Is that all you've been doing at West Point the past few months?" asked Paw.

"They keep us so busy learning to be officers that we don't have time for anything else. We are busy all day learning schoolwork and soldiering."

"You know son, I don't think that boy who called you a down creek Virginia boy knows very much about the flow of water in creeks. We live in the mountains, and water flows downhill to the valleys. According to nature that makes him the down creek boy in more ways than one."

They were all glad to have me home. I told Josh I would help with feeding the hogs. The next morning, after we slopped the hogs, Josh and I went to the barn to help with the milking. While we were milking Paw looked at me.

"Tom, the Junkins raised enough money to buy the mercantile store in town. The whole family works the business and manages to do some farming. Elinor keeps the books, and she takes care of the cash register. Clarksburg is really growing with other businesses starting up. You might think about moving back here to live one of these days. Elinor is a nice looking girl. If it wasn't for taking care of the store and her brothers, she'd be married off."

"I'm glad to hear that Albert and his family are doing so well now. I wander if Al Jr. has rustled anymore hogs?" I wanted to get Paw off the match making business.

"Let bygones be bygones. They're nice and neighborly to us now."

"Maybe I'll see Elinor at church or at the store."

On Saturday, I went directly to Junkin's store to find Elinor behind the counter.

"Tom, I see you're home from West Point."

"I got home a few days ago, and I've been working around the farm helping Maw and Paw with the chores."

"You must come to visit. How about coming this evening? Paw and my brothers would really like seeing you."

"Okay. I'll be there after dinner." I happily returned home to prepare for the evening.

I dressed in my cadet dress uniform, and I walked over to the Junkins that evening. Elinor met me at the door.

"My Tom, don't you look nice in your uniform."

I was embarrassed. I hadn't expected her being so forward.

"Thank you. You look very nice too." Her hair flowed down her back and across her shoulders. She had matured nicely with a nineteen-inch waistline.

She led me into the parlor, and we sat in two rocking chairs facing the fireplace. She added two logs to the fire, and her Paw and brothers came in and greeted me. They were in awe of my uniform, and I could tell Mr. Junkins really liking having me around. The Junkins boys wanted to know all about the Academy so I told them about firing the cannons, riding and musketry. They were more interested in the cannons. I told them in detail the firing of each cannon, and the experiment I ran with varying the size of the powder load. They couldn't get their fill of West Point stories. They had rather hear Academy stories than stories of squirrel hunting. I never knew any young boy in Clarksburg who didn't like a good squirrel-hunting story, and I told West Point stories all evening. The evening had disappeared, and it was time to go. Elinor escorted me to the steps, and I stepped down onto the first step holding onto the banister looking at her.

"Tom, I really enjoy getting your letters. Their contents express your loneliness. I hope my letters make you happy."

"They do. Maw's letters make me feel better also."

"Would you like to go to church with me tomorrow? It's going to snow, and we could stroll to church in the snow."

"Sure, I'll be here early so we can arrive on time."

I was there in dress uniform, and we strolled to church in the snow. Everyone in church was looking at me, and the older people asked many questions wanting to know what I was doing. An elderly lady asked me if I was an officer, and did I know General Winfield Scott. I explained I was only a cadet, and I would become a second lieutenant at graduation. After church we rode the wagon back home, and Elinor and I sat on the back of the wagon allowing our feet to occasionally touch the snow. Maw prepared another one of her great dinners and everyone ate well. Elinor helped clean the dishes from the table then everyone retired to our favorite places in front of the fireplace. After making small talk it was time to take Elinor home. The snow continued to fall all the way to her house, and she invited me in to warm at the fireplace. She added more logs, and the fire was roaring. In a short time I was warm, and it had grown dark. I opened the door to go outside and Elinor followed. Once on the first step I turned to Elinor, and she clutched my hand. It was automatic and I kissed her without thinking about it. I was glad I had been practicing with Millie back at the Academy. Elinor wasn't surprised, and she welcomed the encounter.

"Tom, how much time do you have before you go back to the Academy? I want see you again, and I'll prepare dinner for you."

I assured her I would spend time with her and have dinner before I went back. I trudged through the snow all the way home. It was a wet snow, and my shoes were wet when I got home so I placed them in front of the fireplace to dry. Paw was sitting at the fireplace when I arrived. Everyone had gone to bed, and I sat down beside him.

"Paw, there's one West Point story I haven't told you. There's a farm located next to the Academy, and the farmer has goats. Some of the nannies came into heat. The Academy's mascot, a billy goat named Sarge, sensed the nannies' conditions and reacted with natural baying every night for a week. One night, we took old Sarge to Farmer O'Malley's for a visit. After we turned him loose in the pasture he satisfied the nannies' desires, and then he wanted to stay with them. When we tried to bring him back to the Academy he chased us around the pasture for an hour until we roped him. It took everyone in the barracks to pull him back to the Academy. We were able to sleep after Sarge and the nannies were happy and quiet."

Paw laughed, "I knew you were learning something there. You're learning more than what they're teaching in books."

I slopped the hogs the next morning and this made Josh happy. I had taken over that task after the first day. Josh liked everything about farming except feeding the hogs. I couldn't be a farmer for my life was destined to a greater cause.

My experiences at the Academy were exciting, and I tried to motivate Josh in that direction but he wasn't interested. Sam, the plow mare, had failed in his case. She didn't work him hard enough to convince him to leave the farm.

I was really enjoying my visit home and Maw's cooking. I hadn't realized how much I had missed it. Elinor and her Paw treated me special. In fact, Mr. Junkins liked parading around on the large porch in front of his mercantile business with his hand on my shoulder. A six months trip to the Academy had made me well known in Clarksburg.

Christmas was a joyous time at our house, and Maw prepared a gigantic dinner. We attended church, and Elinor entertained me at her house in the evening. We were developing a fondness for each other; however, she spent so much time preparing meals for her brothers and Paw that there was little time for us. Most of the evening I discussed the Academy with her Paw and brothers. My furlough days evaporated one after the other. New Years Day was another joyous celebration with everyone shooting flintlocks into the air. We had another good chicken dinner, and I spent the evening again with Elinor. After I got home that night I pulled my train ticket from my pocket to see when I would catch the returning train. It left Clarksburg ten o'clock on Saturday morning. I had two more days relieving Josh of the hog slopping duties.

The train ride back was less exciting than the first trip. I wore my Academy daily wear without the sulfur smell for Maw had removed the smell with her strong lye soap. I met Hiram in Pittsburgh same as before. He was in good spirits, and he related that his fathers tannery business was doing well in Cincinnati. His younger brothers were becoming valuable assets to his Paw. One thing that didn't change was Hiram went to sleep again before dinner. Our tickets included dinner, and we ate well. We arrived late at the Academy on Sunday night, and after unpacking we went to bed. Monday was unusually easy allowing us to recover from the return travel. That evening after dinner the cadets casually gathered at the large round table in front of the fireplace. Hill turned toward me with a smile.

"Tom, you should have been with Butler and me the last two days in New York."

Butler joined in, "Yea, Tom, we went to Roses on Church Street, and for two dollars you can have any girl in the house. Hill was the first to pick one, and you should have seen her. She had long hair, big tits, long legs and a sizable behind, and mine had a sizable behind which was nice to hold."

Hill added, "James's girl had plenty behind to hold onto and some left over."

All the cadets had gained interest by now and were listening intensely.

Hill continued, "I guess this was our phase two of becoming a gentleman. Old Butler disappeared upstairs with his girl, and I didn't see him for hours. I found a room on the first floor by the parlor, and I must have made love to her at least five times. She was difficult to satisfy, and I thought I would be there all night."

"Did you get her name, A.P.?" James asked.

"Now James, do those girls have names? I didn't give her my name either. All I would need is for her to show up here looking for me."

McClellan entered the barracks and Butler repeated the Roses escapade, and McClellan looked shocked.

"Gentlemen, you won't be expecting me to join you at Roses. The Academy gave you good advice to stay away from there." From that time on McClellan minimized the time he spent with Hill and Butler. He formed a stronger friendship with George Custer. McClellan turned toward Hiram.

"Well Grant, what did you do over the break?"

"I helped Paw and my brothers with the tannery. Paw is expanding the business in Kentucky. We can get cheaper labor from those northern Kentucky farm boys. They work harder too."

"How about you, Tom?"

"I enjoyed the vacation and holidays with the family." I was dying to tell about Elinor but held it within myself.

"You mean you didn't see the girlfriend while you were home?"

"I saw a friend that's a girl."

Longstreet came alive, "Yea, what's the difference between a girlfriend and a friend that's a girl?" Everyone laughed.

Jeb, Sherm and Rosecran sat quietly absorbing the conversation of the evening. Jeb added the remaining coals to the fireplace, and he and Sherm refilled the coal buckets and banked the fireplaces for the night. The next day we began our reviews for our exams. Artillery and musketry classes were used to clean and restore our weapons. The exams were to begin that Monday, and artillery and musketry exam would consist of shooting, equipment maintenance and cleaning the firearms. The remainder of the week my time was spent studying and reviewing literature, mathematics and Natural Philosophy. Everyone spent Saturday night studying instead of going to Benny Havens.

The next week was a really difficult time period, and my literature exam was on Monday. Mathematics exam was Tuesday, and Natural Philosophy exam was Wednesday. Thursday and Friday I would finish up with musketry and artillery, respectively. Grades were posted on Saturday, and we were given the rest of the day off. By this time everyone was ready to celebrate. Saturday, I was up early anxious to see my grade. The grades were posted in Monroe Hall, and I was the first there. I eagerly reviewed the list to find I had passed all classes with low marks. My higher marks were in artillery and musketry, and I ranked next to the bottom of the class. George Custer saved me from being the bottom. He had failed Literature and had to repeat the class. Hiram passed all classes ranking thirty-second. Everyone came back to the barracks, and we celebrated after breakfast.

Monday morning we registered for class. I had completed my Literature requirement so I registered for Natural Philosophy, Mathematics, Chemistry, Artillery and Musketry. Fortunately Mosby had registered for chemistry, and I had someone to study with.

We were wakened early Tuesday Morning by a painful groan from A.P.

"Oh, Oh, I hurt."

"What's wrong, Hill?" asked Butler.

"I'm hurting in the groin, and I can't urinate."

"You'd better see the doctor."

"I guess I'll have to. It hurts too bad for me to attend class."

"Will you go with me?"

"I'd go with you, but I have a class at eight o'clock."

"How about you, Rosecran?"

"I have a class also, A.P."

I spoke up, "I'll go with you. My first period is free. The doctor comes in at eight."

"Thanks, Tom."

Everyone went to class, and I took Hill to the doctor. We were the first to arrive at his office so the doctor saw us immediately. The agony on Hill's face indicated the pain was getting worse.

"What can I do for you boys?" the doctor asked.

Hill immediately spoke, "I've got this pain in the groin, and it been getting worse all morning."

"Do you have problems urinating?"

Hill replied, "Yes, it hurts."

"Have you been doing anything you shouldn't have been doing?"

"What do you mean?" Hill inquired.

"You know what I mean. We initially tell all cadets to stay out of the bordellos at the beginning of the year, and I think they interpret this as an invitation to visit there. Annually, after the Christmas furlough I usually have two or three returning for the treatment. So, now, tell me if you had relations with questionable females."

"Yes." Hill replied.

Turning toward me, "How about you?"

"No. I came along to bring him here."

"You can wait outside."

I waited outside and listened to the remainder of A. P.'s exam.

"Okay. Tell me your name and the details. Where have you been?" asked the doctor.

"My name is Ambrose Hill, and I am a first year cadet. I came back to the Academy two days early to see New York City. The last night I visited Church Street."

"Where did you go on Church Street?"

"A place called Roses."

"The famous Roses. Her place has educated many West Point cadets."

"What's the lady's name you were with?"

"I didn't ask her name."

"Well, Ambrose. It doesn't matter. She wouldn't have given you her real name anyway. Let's see what we can do for you. I'll give you this elixir to take three times a day. I'll see you next Tuesday to determine your progress. The elixir will relieve some of your pain. You must inform the other members of your barracks that you have a venereal disease. You must use separate bathing facilities to prevent the spread of the disease. In fact, if you spread the disease, you'll be expelled. A long-term effect of the disease is prostatitis. We'll continue treatment and try to curb this problem. Do you have any questions?"

"No, Thank you, sir."

We departed the infirmary returning to the barracks in time for me to attend my first Chemistry class. The class began with the definition of chemistry and the Periodic Table of Elements, and we were given two lists of elements to memorize. One list contained cations with positive valences, and the other list was anions with negative valences. Mosby and I practiced the memory work back in the barracks. Studying the memory work paid off the next day when we recited the cations and anions for a quiz. We didn't understand the applications of the memory work until a month later when we began studying compounds. It was an interesting subject, and we continued to study hoping to better understand the concepts and applications.

I penned two letters to Elinor and the family by firelight. I didn't want to use valuable daylight for writing letters. I told Elinor how much I enjoyed visiting with her, and that maybe we could do it again at my next furlough in June. I told them I was doing well and had added Chemistry to my other classes.

The Chemistry class was becoming more interesting as we spent an entire class on gunpowder. Gunpowder was made from equal portions of potassium nitrate, sulfur and graphite. When the charge was ignited as in a gun, there were instantly formed gases of nitrogen, sulfur and carbon. Accompanying the gases was an enormous energy given off by the formation of sulfur dioxide, carbon dioxide, and nitrogen trioxide. The energy and gas volume reacted on the surrounding housing of the gun forcing a projectile through the gun's muzzle. The reaction was referred to as an oxidation reaction. I took notes for later recall for this was another class with practical applications. Now I understood the reason why cutting the cannon charge in half produced a distance of approximately one-third of a full charge in my first artillery class. There wasn't enough gases and energy to force the projectile to half the distance.

Hill humbly informed everyone of his condition. He moaned in his sleep at night, and everyone was sympathetic. He missed all his classes and drills the next day. He faithfully took his elixir, and it began to take effect the third day. He was able to attend class, but he missed the drills. Butler was spending less time in his company for he didn't want the disease associated with him.

The latest national news reports highlighted the turncoat Santa Anna's activities. Santa Anna's ravage of The Alamo was discussed in detail during evening discussions around the barracks fireplaces. It was also dissected in our artillery and musketry classes. It was a futile defense of a fortified church in Saint Antonio by Colonel Travis, Jim Bowie and Davy Crockett. There were approximately two hundred Texans defending The Alamo against three thousand of Santa Anna's Mexicans. Eventually the Mexicans wiped out Travis's only cannon, and they overran the defense laying waste to all inhabitants.

The week dragged on with Hill regaining enough composure to attend all classes and drills. Saturday night came and everyone was off to Benny Havens Tavern except Hill. We arrived at the tavern before the music started so we played billiards and drank beer. I searched the establishment for Millie, but she wasn't there. The music started, and I noticed Butler and McClellan disappearing outside with their girls. I spotted Hill's girl sitting with two other girls at a centrally located table, and as I strolled by the table on the way to the bar, she waved for my attention.

"Aren't you Tom?" she inquired.

"Yes, Tom Jackson."

"My name is Mary Beth Hopkins. You might have seen me here with Ambrose Hill. He told me your name along with some of the other cadets. Where is Ambrose anyway?"

"Hill decided to devote the evening to his studies."

"How unusual. He doesn't normally have to study to pass his classes."

As I started to depart to the billiards parlor she clutched my arm, "Would you dance with me?"

She was a pretty girl, and I didn't want to leave her without a partner.

"Sure, next jig."

We danced a jig and a waltz. We drank beer, and we danced another jig and waltz. She grew prettier as the evening got shorter. Had the evening lasted longer with our growing urges we may have gone outside for some hugging and kissing. I was getting better at kissing all the time, and it appeared the more I kissed was the more I wanted to kiss. We bid each other good evening, and I returned to the barracks. On the way back Longstreet turned to me laughing.

"Tom, what are you going to tell Hill?"

"The truth. I'll tell him she asked about him."

"At what point did she ask? Was it between the waltz and the beer or the jig and the waltz?"

"Well, you know she's a perfectly good girl, and I didn't want to see her go to waste. We just had a good time."

We finally reached the barracks and found Hill asleep. The last few days he had been sleeping better. We went to bed without much commotion. My head hardly touched the pillow, and the next thing I knew it was Sunday morning. On Monday we were having drills next to O'Malley farm. The horses, cows and goats were grazing in the pasture, and the three nannies were obviously in a motherly way. They would be delivering almost any day.

I received a letter from Elinor, and I had saved it to read by the fireplace light when I had more privacy. She related the status of the mercantile business and how busy it kept her. Albert had been talking about me visiting the business and her at home. She expressed the special feeling of us being together while I was there on Christmas furlough.

We had studied many practical mathematical applications now. We were studying logarithms, and there were many pages of data to use for logarithm computation. I developed a shortcut method to approximate the correctness of my logarithmic answer. I had to compute easy examples to develop the shortcut technique. The method employed the definition of logarithms of numbers ending in zero. The logarithm of 0 is zero, of 10 is one, of 100 is two and of 1000 is three. I theorized the logarithm of a number between any of these numbers could be estimated with some degree of accuracy. For example, the logarithm of 333 would be 2.xxx. It was only an approximation, but it helped me be confident in my exam answers.

The weeks started to roll by again, and O'Malleys nannies gave birth to three kids. Sarge occasionally brayed his approval for his offsprings. We continued to mature in our training, and Hill kept regular weekly appointments with the doctor. He continued to use his medication three times a day. The disease had infected his prostate to a degree, and sometimes it was difficult for him to sit. He had missed more classes, and he had not been to the tavern since we returned from furlough. His marks had dropped significantly from the period before Christmas furlough. He had not asked about Mary Beth, and I had been making sure she didn't get lonely. It was Saturday again, and we went to Ben Havens Tavern. Butler and his girl were having much discussion, and they did not go outside all evening. I played billiards, and joined Mary Beth at the bar. We drank beer, danced and went outside for other entertainment, and as usual the evening was too short.

On Wednesday there was much excitement in Monroe Hall at the Colonel's office. Butler's Saturday night girl was there with her father, and her father made claims to the Colonel that his daughter was pregnant. James Butler had impregnated his daughter. Butler was summoned, and the inquisition by the Colonel followed. James confessed to the circumstance in a gentlemanly fashion. Two days later James was suspended from the Academy, and he returned to Charlottesville. One month later, he stopped by the Academy entrance for a short visit on his way to his wedding in New York City. Hill had a lengthy conversation with him at the Academy gate. A week later Hill was best man at Butler's wedding. It was the last time Hill would ever see Butler.

Hill continued to have painful bouts with his prostate, and Hiram was beginning to drink in the barracks again. Mosby was moving nearer to the top of the class, and Custer remained at the bottom. I continued to study at every opportunity except the Saturday evenings I was with Mary Beth. Had Hill known what he was missing he would have never gone to Roses.

The month of April began with a twelve-inch snow, and it was Friday evening free time to play in the snow. We snowballed and rolled each other, and we made a makeshift sled, which we pulled it to the top of a nearby hill and rode it until it fell apart. We were exhausted, and when we returned to the barracks we made large coal fires in both fireplaces to dry our coats and clothing. It was times like this we enjoyed the Academy as being more than a school and a military institution. It was the replacement of our home life. Even with its strict requirements I appreciated the education and opportunity it afforded me. I had access to many books, and I was developing daily into the military man I had aspired to. If I had the opportunity to relive my mortal life again, I would repeat this period again even with all its emotional trials.

Graduation came at the end of May. Lee and McClellan graduated, and they were commissioned second lieutenants in the army. Lee graduated with honors having been the only cadet to graduate without a demerit. Lee was assigned to General Winfield Scott's command, and McClellan was assigned to General Zachary Taylor unit.

It was time for our summer furlough, and I returned to the farm and mill in Clarksburg. Paw picked me up with the buggy at the train. He had acquired a tobacco base to add to our farming activities, and I would be there for a month to help with the chores of growing tobacco. I renewed the task of slopping the hogs. June apples were in abundance this year, and I fed them to the hogs. The hogs loved these tart-tasting apples. I liked the green apples for they reminded me of the sour lemons at the Academy Mess Hall. Maw and the family were glad to see me again. The luster had worn off my second visit home, and everyone I met in Clarksburg asked if I were home on furlough again.

An iron mill was the new economic addition to Clarksburg. There had been a large magnetite deposit discovered at a coal-mining site. The abundance of coal, water and now iron ore was the combination needed to produce low-grade iron, and the iron mill employed two hundred Clarksburg residents. The iron was used to build home heating stoves and furnaces. The water was used to treat the ore residue, and it served as a cooling agent in the heat-treating operation. The water carried waste residues from the new smelting operation and deposited them in the river basins.

The new tobacco base required a great deal of time in soil preparation, and it was a finicky crop. It had to be planted, hoed, pruned and wormed. All this was performed prior to harvesting and curing. The tobacco worming was fun. We found and hand removed three-inch green tobacco worms from each plant. The worms were harmless to people, but they could ruin a good tobacco crop. Once they were removed from the plant we placed them on the ground. Then we stepped on them squirting worm juices in all directions. I spent my June furlough working this one-acre tobacco base.

The spring flowers were at their peak in Clarksburg, and the pear, cherry and red bud trees were in full bloom. The spring rain and sunshine had performed magic on the mountains and hills around Clarksburg. It was a furlough I greatly enjoyed with my Maw, Paw, brothers and sisters. My weekend evenings were spent in town at Albert's mercantile business or with Elinor on her front porch swing.

Again the furlough was over too soon, and on July fifth I boarded the train to West Point. I arrived there two days later ready to begin studies and drills again. I visited Little Sorrell after unpacking, and I took her for a ride and curried her. I could tell she had missed me while I was away. Everyone returned except A. P. Hill, and it was reported that he was taking a leave due to his prostatitis problem. His family physician submitted a plea for his one-year leave of absence in order to cure his problem.

There was a new class of recruits, and it was time for O'Malley's nannies to come in heat again. These cadets came from New York, Maine and Pennsylvania, and they did not understand Sarge's baying desires. We had to explain it to them, and we explained in great detail how to solve the problem. They finally understood the requirement to relieve Sarge's natural urges, and it was a hilarious event. They roped Sarge, and three cadets pulled him to O'Malley's farm. Their problem began when they were unable to bring Sarge home. They finally gave up until one of the new cadets rushed into our barracks to get Sherm's help. Sherm woke me laughing.

"Tom, we must help these new cadets get Sarge home."

"We did our time with Sarge last year."

"Yea, I know but these boys can't do the job this year."

With that explanation we were on our way to O'Malley's farm to retrieve Sarge. We arrived at the farm to find Sarge still chasing the nannies. All the cadets stormed the pasture, and Sarge chased them until he was exhausted. Sherm and I finally roped him, and the cadets wrestled him back to the Academy stall. John Mosby had been promoted into Lee's sergeant position, and he was there to give us the gentlemen's speech.

"Tom and Sherm, what are you doing with these new cadets on Sarge's annual adventure?"

Sherm replied, "John, you're not going to believe these new cadets. They took old Sarge over to O'Malley's and couldn't get him home. They returned to the barracks to get Tom and me to help."

Mosby laughed, "I guess we're going to have a lot of training with these new recruits."

He proceeded giving the speech Lee delivered to us a year earlier, but he did not mention the demerit parts. He had received a few demerits last year for using the coal pile in an ungentlemanly way.

By the time Saturday night had come, the new cadets had already found Benny Havens Tavern. They were more accustomed to these establishments than the previous class. The cadets were welcoming the local girls on every occasion, and I reacquainted myself with Mary Beth. Mary Beth and I were enjoying the evening when I heard a familiar voice from the past.

"Why hello, Tom." said Millie Johnson.

"Hello, Millie." I said casually. "How have you been?"

"Who's she?" asked Mary Beth.

"She an old friend I met here last year." Sensing I was in an uncomfortable predicament I began thinking what a West Point gentlemen would do to diminish the stress.

"Millie and I met last year." Mary Beth was beginning to show her green eyes, and I decided to take the situation in hand.

"Mary Beth, I would like to introduce you to Millie. And Millie, this is Mary Beth. Mary Beth and I are spending the evening dancing."

The introduction was enough to send Millie on her way, and we didn't see her again. We danced and later went outside for other activities. Apparently I had managed the situation in a gentlemanly fashion; however, Millie never spoke to me again. Later that night before going to sleep I recall the situation.

The next night I started a new nightly ritual exercise to help circulate my blood. It required me to stand upside down on my hands with my head toward the floor and my feet resting against the wall. I performed this exercise for five minutes each night while other cadets gathered to watch me.

Longstreet commented, "What's Crazy Tom doing now?"

"I'm redistributing my blood."

The mess hall had received another shipment of citrus, and now I could get all the lemons I wanted. I managed to bring a couple to the barracks every night. I had missed getting my citrus while I was on furlough.

I received a letter and a small package from Maw and Paw, and the letter was about the tobacco crop. The base had produced eighteen hundred pounds of tobacco, and Williamsons Tobacco Company made a fourteen cents a pound market bid for it. This was a small fortune for Maw and Paw. Maw bought material to sew dresses for her and the girls, and Paw bought new shoes for everyone that school year. The small package was a pound of home grown tobacco, which I stored in the desk.

The next night everyone sat on the porch benches, and Sherm looked over at me.

"Tom, what did you receive in that package from home yesterday?"

"Maw and Paw sent me some tobacco from our first crop. You know the tobacco I helped plant and cultivate while on the June furlough."

"Where is it?" asked Hiram.

"It's in my desk."

"Go get it." Longstreet demanded.

I retrieved it from the desk.

"I've never seen tobacco in that form." Stated Rosecran. "Does one chew or smoke it?"

"Either way or both." Replied Jeb Stuart taking a leaf and wadding it into his jaw. Sherm, Hiram, Longstreet and I followed suit.

"Come on, Rosecran, have a little chew. It won't hurt you."

"Okay, Jeb, but if I get sick I'll never forgive you."

By now we were working the tobacco to a good spit, and we let it fly off the porch. Rosecran produced a small squirt to join the gang. We continued to talk and spit for another five minutes when we noticed Rosecran getting sick. He was turning green, and all of a sudden he began to regurgitate. He was one sick cadet, and we gave him water to rinse the tobacco from his mouth and to dilute the tobacco acid in his stomach. Everyone felt sympathy for him, but we still laughed. Just as we were getting ready to remove the tobacco from our mouths Mosby appeared.

"What are you boys doing there?"

Everyone was trying to hide the chewing tobacco.

"Tom, what's that in you mouth?"

"It something Maw sent me from home."

"Ah pshaw, either your Maw sent you some tobacco or some bad cooking. And with all this tobacco spit and tobacco smell I'd have to say it must be tobacco. In short, if it looks like tobacco and smell like tobacco, it must be tobacco."

Hiram could hold back no longer, "Well, John, you've caught us. Are you giving us demerits? If you had been with us, you'd had some to."

"Nay, Hiram, I'm not giving you demerits. Take it easy on poor old Rosecran. You know he's not used to raw tobacco from the curing barn. He's probably only used refined honey tobacco. You boys go to bed. Maybe tonight's rain will wash away the ambeer."

We saluted and said goodnight. Rosecran had recovered and we went to bed. I would savor this experience to tell Paw. I knew he would really enjoy this story. The next day I penned Paw a letter about Mexico, the annexation of Texas and the upcoming election.

14 September 1845

Dear Paw,

I'm writing you this letter to inform you of the news here at the Academy. It appears the Mexican government has been upset with the Republic of Texas since Sam Houston defeated Mexico at the Battle of San Jacinto. Even though the Mexicans signed the Treaty of Velasco, they do not recognize Texas as an independent republic. The Mexican government repudiated the treaty and considered Texas to be a rebellious Mexican territory. There is also a dispute about the southern border of Texas. Mexico says it's Rio Nueces and Texas claims it's the Rio Grande. The United States government recognizes Texas's independence, and has offered terms of annexation as a state, which it accepted this past July. Mexico has threatened to invade Texas. Gen. Zachary Taylor has been commissioned to thwart any attempt at an invasion by stationing his troops in Corpus Christi.

It appears James K. Polk may be elected president in the November election, and the Academy supports him being elected. He is a protégé of Andrew Jackson, and they say he believes in expanding the United States. However, he is more refined and does not duel like Old Hickory.

I have to study Chemistry now. We're studying oxidation-reduction equations.

Give Maw and the children my love.

Your son,

Tom

The weekend was approaching fast, and we had been busy with all the Academy's classes, drills and activities. It was like we only existed from weekend to weekend. There hardly was time to think about the family back home or the girls we met at the tavern. However, we were becoming aware of national issues and their importance.

The New York autumn countryside was breathtaking. The leaves increased sugar content had made their color intense. This year the reds were redder, the orange seemed more orange and the yellows more yellow than ever before. The colors would only last another month if we had no rain or heavy winds. Later the leaves would accumulate in drifts, and we would walk in them down by the river. The crunching sound beneath our feet always brought us back to reality within the Academy grounds.

Saturday night, we went to Ben Havens Tavern. We played billiards until the music started then Mosby, Longstreet and I looked for our girls, and we found them. We danced and drank until Hiram and Sherm joined us from the card playing room. They both had won tonight, and Grant was especially happy.

"Look, Tom. I won and so did Sherm. I won two hundred dollars. The most money I ever had."

"That's great."

"Do I owe you any money, Tom? Do you want to borrow any money?"

"No." I wanted to say yes for the breakfast I bought him a year ago but thought better of it.

Mary Beth and I wanted to get away from the crowd so we went outside into the trees. The autumn evenings were briskly cool, forcing us to return inside. We danced and made plans to meet during the next week. I had never slipped out of the Academy since the night we took Sarge to Farmer O'Malley. It sounded like it would be fun, and besides, I hadn't received any demerits in months. The meeting was to occur at Benny Havens Wednesday night after lights out. Wednesday night came, and I slipped out through the window Hill had used a year earlier. I ran past O'Malley's farm to the tavern, and I had broken a good sweat running. There was an excitement of slipping out and meeting Mary Beth. I was twenty minutes early, and was beginning to cool off. By the time Mary Beth arrived I was getting cold in the late autumn evening air.

"Tom, Tom." She called as she came around the corner of Ben Havens Tavern.

"Here I am." I said as I stood leaning against the porch post.

We embraced, and immediately we headed toward our passion spot in the woods. The passion was furious, and I continued getting cold from the sweat and cool air.

Mary Beth looked up at me. "Did you bring a coat?"

"No. I was in a hurry to get away. I had to leave after lights out."

"I'm getting cold."

"Me too." The body heat wasn't enough to ward off the cold bitter evening. "Maybe we should go home and meet Saturday night."

"Sounds like an evening arrangement to me."

We kissed and were on our way. I started running once she was out of sight, and I made it back to the barracks in record time. I had broken a sweat again even in the chilling air. No one was visible, and I slipped over the wall and into the barracks through the same window I had exited earlier.

"I see you made it," said Hiram.

"Did anyone miss me?"

"Just me." Jeb tuned in.

Mosby started laughing.

"Goodnight, boys."

Mary Beth and I met at Ben Havens Tavern that Saturday night as we continued to do ever Saturday night for the next few months. During this time I had received many letters from Elinor and the family. I always found time to reply to everyone. Elinor continued to express her fondness, and I always returned her compliment. At this time in my life I did not seriously consider females in my future. My time was now, and I had no idea of the future. My study habits improved, and my class participation and grades were reflecting my learning. I understood the oxidation-reduction concept of the chemical equations. Natural Philosophy remained my favorite subject, and I struggled with accepting the mathematical concept of imaginary numbers being real numbers. After accepting the concept it made perfect sense. It was the only way possible to square root a negative number.

I returned home again for the December furlough, and I resumed slopping the hogs again. Josh was grateful for December was a cold month in the Clarksburg hills to go out for early morning feedings. Sometimes, I added hot water to the frozen slop before giving it to the hogs. The family enjoyed a merry Christmas from the tobacco crop profits, and everyone received new shoes and outfits. My brothers and sisters were really growing up, and they were becoming young men and women.

My furlough was over and I returned to the Academy. My studies continued to add an extra dimension to my life. I always added coals to the fireplace near my bed and desk so I could continue to study after the coal oil lamps were ordered out. I had risen in my class academic standing at the end of my third term. I was half way through the educational task I started a year and a half ago, and I continue to be motivated by my desire to receive a college education. I was learning much from textbooks; however, I was learning equally from my classmates and professors in our social gatherings. This was a routine term, which passed very fast, and my standing improved again. I went home again to visit the family and Elinor.

Upon returning to West Point I found that my friend Ambrose had returned to finish his education. His prostate ailment was in remission, and he was much more subdued and cordial now. He and Nathan Hull were given a separate room for their accommodations. The room turned into a hangout for other cadets to smoke tobacco. Hill and Hull led everyone for receiving the most demerits. They were given demerits for snowball fights, misuse of the coal pile and slipping out of the Academy at night. They set the record for receiving the most demerits given to anyone at the Academy.

The first Saturday night back we went to Benny Havens Tavern. I was seated with Mary Beth and Ambrose joined us.

"How have you been, Mary Beth?" he inquired.

"Oh, Ambrose, I've been very well. Tom has been keeping me company while you've been gone."

I could tell she really enjoyed seeing him again. At that moment I felt someone's hand on my shoulder. I turned to find Mary Morrison, and I didn't know if I was in a predicament or not.

"How have you been, Tom?" she asked.

"I'm fine and where have you been for about a year?"

"Aren't you going to introduce me to your friends?"

"Sure, you remember Ambrose Hill. And this is Mary Beth."

"Oh sure, I remember both of them."

"I remember you too." Ambrose spoke up.

"Are you and Tom still involved?"

"Well, I've been away for about a year."

"Must have been a convenient year for everyone. How are we going to work this out Tom?" Ambrose asked jokingly. "Maybe we could have us a duel with the Academy's cannons."

I could tell it was Mary Beth's turn. She looked at me and I realized it could never be with us.

"Maybe I can work it out for you two and prevent a cannon duel. Tom, I didn't realize you and Mary Morrison were involved when we met. Maybe we can just stop time for a year and go back to the time where we were a year ago."

"Well, Mary Beth, I never kept Mary Morrison a secret. It appears you want to be with Ambrose. If Mary is happy to become reacquainted we'll continue with the party. Would you like to dance Miss Mary?"

"Sure, Tom, let's dance the way we use to dance."

We danced and partied all evening until it was time to return to the barracks. Mary had been in the city taking care of a sick relative for the past year. Her relative was better now, and she promised to return to Ben Havens Tavern the next Saturday night. I could hardly wait for I thought about her all week. It finally came, and it was the longest week I had spent at the Academy. I dispensed with going to the billiards parlor when I entered the Tavern. Instead I spent the time looking for Mary, and I found her. We danced, and after a few dances we went outside to the area, which had become known as the passion pit. It didn't take long for us to become reacquainted. She had an irresistible spirit within her, and she brought out desires within me like no other girl that I had ever known. Elinor was much too timid to make me have those feelings. I continued to see Mary every Saturday night. We never tired of each other's company for she stirred a passion within me. My desire to procure an education was the only factor making me remain at the Academy and not leaving to pursue a life with Mary Morrison. Ambrose and Mary Beth became a familiar couple again, and we shared a table often at the tavern. Hill had become a more tolerable individual now that he had definite graduation goals.

Our barracks was the first to develop the custom of using candles to study by after lights were out. It was my last year, and I wanted to make sure I graduated. The commandant probably knew of our studying by candlelight, but he ignored giving demerits for studying after lights were out.

I wrote a letter to Paw. He always liked the news coming from the Academy.

1846, October

Dear Paw,

We've declared war on Mexico. It appears I'll be going there after I graduate. I can hardly wait to show Santa Anna what I've learned to do with a cannon. I wish we had some of the new cannons they're currently developing for ships. Paw, the cannons are so big that we haven't developed a method to withstand the repercussion of the guns on land. Only a ship can withstand these repercussions, which are absorbed by the water.

The United States is supporting the Republic of Texas against the aggression of Mexico. Mexico is denying the rights of the Texas people to become citizens of the United States. We are defending the rights of the Texans to choose their own destiny. Paw, if I go to war against Mexico, there will be many opportunities for promotions, and I am trained and capable of performing the tasks of war.

Everyone at the Academy supports President Polk's decision in going to war with Mexico. Many cadets still talk of the brave Tennessee Volunteers who died at the Alamo with Sam Houston. We will avenge these men when given the opportunity, and I can do things with these cannons that will make those Mexicans sorry they attacked the Alamo.

The family is growing up fast without me. Tell Maw and everyone hello for me and give them my love.

Your son,

Tom

Hill and Hull received more demerits for tobacco in their room. They were caught smoking and chewing, and it seemed they couldn't get enough of it. Hiram was hitting the bottle again. He no longer pursued the activity of female company at the Tavern. He and Sherm spent their Saturday nights in the back room playing cards.

The next two months past and I went home again for the December furlough. I didn't realize it but it would be my last visit home as a bachelor. As usual I took over the hog feeding for Josh, and it was my last period slopping those animals. My last morning's feeding I lingered after putting the slop in the trough. It was as if I had developed a bond feeding them. I caught the train later that day to return to the Academy, and I didn't visit Elinor this furlough for I had missed Mary. It had become old hat for the family to see me return to the Academy, and it was no longer a celebration at the train when I returned.

When I returned to West Point the grades were posted, and I had increased my class standing. I occupied the twenty-fifth position. Custer remained at the bottom of the class, and Mosby, Hiram and Sherm maintained their class rankings. It was back to intense studies, carrying coal for the fireplaces and having fun at Benny Havens Tavern. The first Saturday night back at Ben Havens Tavern Mary mentioned I should meet her parents. I dismissed the thought, and we went directly to the passion woods. It was a cold January night, and the passion was great but the environment was too cold. We returned inside to get warm, and after we were warm we danced the evening away. The next Saturday night I returned to Benny Havens Tavern to find Mary waiting with her parents.

"Hello, Tom."

"Hello, Mary. Who's with you?"

"Tom, I want you to meet my parents. This is my mother Rosemary Morrison and my father Stanfill Morrison." Turning to her parents, "This is Thomas Jackson from Clarksburg, Virginia. He's the cadet I've been telling you about."

Her mother nodded and her father spoke, "My name is Stanfill Morrison spelled with two l's. At home I'm sometimes referred to as Col. Stanfill Morrison."

"Very happy to meet you." I said, thinking Morrison is spelled with two R's.

"Glad to see our Mary has taken up with a military man. The military is a good future for a man. The war should produce opportunity for advancement for a young cadet."

"I'm looking forward to serving the cause for freeing the Texas Republic. Have you ordered anything?"

"No, we haven't. Mary has had us waiting for you. Order anything you want. I know cadets have a limited income, and the evening is on me."

The evening was a long one with the Colonel having too much to drink, and I paid the check, which took a half-month's pay. We danced the evening away, and we spent no time in the passion pit. The Morrisons invited me to visit their house in the City. I told them the Academy did not allow us to leave the compound except for Saturday night. Rosemary kept telling me how nice it was to meet me, and she wanted to know all about Clarksburg, the farm and the hogs.

We said our goodnights, and I agreed to meet Mary there again next weekend. Hopefully, without her parents for I doubt if I'm ever as smart as the Colonel think he is.

Sunday, I wrote Paw another letter.

1845, January

Dear Paw,

President Polk has moved General Zachary Taylor from Rio Nueces to north of the Rio Grande. The general has taken up a defensive position on the north side of the river. His army set up a supply depot and constructed fieldwork across from Matamoros. The Mexican commander in Matamoros demanded Gen. Taylor to withdraw his troops. Taylor responded saying he takes his orders from the president of the United States and not some Mexican officer. The Mexican general informed Gen. Taylor that he considered this to be a hostile action. Gen. Taylor replied saying this was not a hostile action, but the hostile action would be whoever fired the first shot and he did not intend to do so.

The Mexican government is circulating letters claiming the American soldiers were fighting against other fellow Catholics. The letters also promise parcels of Mexican land for those willing to desert to join the Mexican Army. Gen. Taylor responded by ordering anyone caught swimming the Rio Grande to Mexico shot. The Mexican general increased his army at Matamoros to twice its size. In response, Gen. Taylor men named their earthwork entrenchment Fort Texas.

In a few months I'll be finishing here at the Point. I'm looking forward to my next assignment. Everyone wants an opportunity to participate in the war.

Give everyone my best regards. Tell Josh to keep slopping those hogs. Hope your tobacco base is profitable again this year.

Your son,

Tom

Later that day as we gathered around the fireplace, Custer asked.
"How did the Mexican War get started?"
"It started when Texas declared its independence from Mexico, and the United States annexed Texas in 1845." Mosby responded.
"Why do we want Texas?" Custer asked.
"Polk wants to expand the American borders, and he's under pressure to increase the number of slave states. In order to gain support on his expansion program he is forced to be liberal in granting the new states the right to have slavery." Said Mosby. He knew all the answers to the questions.
George was satisfied with Mosby's explanations. We could've told Custer the Mexican War was between the United States and the French, and he would've believed it. He was just happy to be here.
The days were flying by. It was Saturday evening and time to go to Ben Havens Tavern again. I met Mary early and we danced. I held her small slender fingers, and I experienced the fragrance of her hair. We went outside to the passion woods, and I tasted her sweet lips and caressed her bosoms with my body. Life was great, and the passion grew until we could stand it no longer. We

returned inside the tavern. We danced again and again. The ale increased our sensitivity, but the evening was over. I returned to the barracks to entertain a sleepless night, and her fragrance haunted me. She was the perfect specimen. She was an example of purity and truth all rolled into one, and I was smitten. I dreamed how the candlelight glistened on her hair.

On Sunday I opened the letter from home I had received earlier in the week. Maw was realizing my maturity, and my time at the Academy would be coming to a close in a few months. She questioned the near future after graduation, and I comforted her by assuring I'd be home for furlough after graduation. She related it was unfortunate that she and Paw were unable to attend graduation. She always sent her love and the family's regards.

January turned into February, and I continued to do well in all my courses and drills. However, I could hardly wait until Saturday night to see Mary, and this Saturday night was special. I met her early and she began.

"Tom, what's your plans after the Academy?"

"I'll become a lieutenant, and I hope to serve in the war."

"Tom, where do I fit into these plans?"

"What do you mean? You're very special to me."

"How special, Tom?"

"Very special. What do you mean?"

"Tom, do you want me in your life after graduation?"

"Yes."

"Tom, that's a start."

"What do you mean? Let's dance."

"No, Tom. We can have our entire life to dance. Can't you understand? We enjoy each other's company, and your education is coming to a close. And the only plan we have is to meet next Saturday night."

"I understand our situation better than you might think. I've been driven the past three years to graduate from West Point. I'm the best artillery man at the Academy, and I think I have a real future in the military."

"I can adapt to the military, and I'll wait for you at home with the children until the war is over."

"Let's talk about it more next Saturday night. I'll sleep on a decision for I have very strong feelings for you."

"You love me?"

"Yeah, I love you."

"That's fine with me. I love you, too. You see that wasn't so hard."

We immediately went to the passion woods, and the passion was never greater. It was so great that I couldn't separate the desire from love, and I was beginning to believe they were the same. The evening was coming to a close, and it was a good thing. I don't believe I could contain the passion any longer, and I didn't realize it yet but plans were being formulated for our future.

Thinking about my future produced another sleepless Saturday night. I realized I had some serious thinking to do, and I realized that I had never contemplated more than having a good time with Mary. She added a new dimension to my life, and when I was with Mary I forgot about everything else. I didn't even know who I was anymore, and I didn't know much about her. She was an Irish girl living in New York City, and she made me feel like no other girl I ever met. The hours with her passed liked minutes, and I must make a decision, which would affect the rest of our lives. I couldn't consult Mosby on a matter of the heart. I think he would tell me that this was my decision anyway, and that any decision would be the right one. It took a whole week for me to conclude to marry Mary. I considered the short-range expenses and the long-range obligations. I didn't even know my responsibilities as a groom. Finally, Saturday night came and I met Mary.

"Here, I am." She motioned to me. Her eyes were sparkling and she was happily laughing.

"Hello, Mary."

"Did you think about us this week?"

"All week long. I couldn't get it off my mind."

"Did you make a decision?"

"I think so. I'm not sure of anything, and I've never experienced anything like this before. I don't even know what to do, and I want you in my life. I want you to know one thing—what you see is what you get. There is no more than the physical me, and what the Academy has made of me."

"Tom, are you saying what I think you're saying? You're making me so happy." She kissed me at the table in the center of Ben Havens Tavern.

"Yes."

"Say it, Tom. Say it."

"Okay. Mary, will you spend the rest of your life with me as Mary Jackson?"

"Yes, Tom. Yes. We must start making wedding plans, and we can be married in the Academy's chapel. Don't worry about wedding expenses for Rosemary and Stanfill will take care of everything."

"Okay." I was worried about that last statement. The last time Stanfill was paying the bill it cost me half months pay.

We went to the passion woods returning to Ben Havens Tavern only when we became too cold. We planned the date to be immediately after graduation. We made many plans including getting the wedding rings. She told me there were many places in the City to buy the wedding bands at a reasonable price, and I was glad she took care of this endeavor. I just realized I had never had a ring before, and I didn't know wedding rings had to be sized.

"We can size your ring by wrapping a string around your finger. The goldsmith can size the ring by wrapping the string around a sizing mandrel." Mary explained.

We found a string and I wrapped it around my finger as she instructed, and I cut it to size with my horse hoof-trimming pocketknife. She placed the string in a folded paper inside her pocket. She instructed me to approach the Academy's commandant to make arrangements for the chapel. My wedding plans were in the initial stage, and things were really beginning to happen now. She said I would have to do it the very next week to insure we got the date we planned for.

Master Joshua Bates had been promoted to the Academy's commandant, and I made arrangements to talk with him the following Monday. I arrived at his office Monday afternoon, and Sergeant Sterling admitted me.

"Master Bates, Thomas Jackson is here for his appointment." Announced Sergeant Sterling.

I saluted and he returned the salute.

"What can I do for you, Tom?"

"I'm here to…"

"Speak up, Tom."

"Sir, I am here to procure the use of the Academy's chapel the Saturday after graduation."

"And what may I ask do you want to use the chapel for?"

"Sir, I have proposed to a young lady, and I want to use the chapel for our marriage ceremony."

"Very well." He laughed. "Every year we have at least one wedding ceremony in that chapel, and I'm surprised this year. I didn't expect it to be you. You may not be aware the Academy supplies a few limited benefits such as decorations and a chaplain. The other necessities you must provide."

"What other necessities do I need?"

"First you need a bride. She'll have parents, bridesmaids and other things women have in a wedding and a reception. You'll need a best man."

"I didn't realize there was so much to getting married."

"There's a book in the library you may want to consult. It explains the responsibilities a groom must provide in a wedding."

"Thank you, Sir. I appreciate your advice. Back home in Clarksburg we were married at the courthouse, at home or a simple church ceremony."

"Tom, I'll have Sergeant Sterling to reserve the Chapel for you for the first Saturday after graduation. You'll be an officer by then. By the way, Congratulations."

"Thank you, Sir." I saluted.

He returned my salute. I returned to the barracks feeling much better and relieved. I prepared to attend my next class.

Saturday night came and I met Mary at Ben Havens Tavern, and she was anxious for the news. I gave her all the details including the chapel decorations. She had gone to the goldsmith to have our wedding bands made. If my string measurement wasn't exact, the goldsmith could resize the ring. She informed me the cost was three dollars each, and I gave her the money. We were excited planning the wedding all evening. I never knew there was so much planning for a wedding.

I wrote Maw and Paw about the wedding. They replied a week later to inform me that they were happy for me but would be unable to attend. The traveling distance was too great, and they were unable to leave the farm, mill and family. I figured the distance to New York City was too much for them to travel. They informed me to have a friend to stand up for me, and they knew I was mature enough to do the right thing. I immediately set about thinking whom I should get to be my best man. I realized instantly that it should be my best friend, John Mosby. He had been a true friend, and I could confide in him. I confided in Mosby at the first opportunity and he agreed to stand up for me. He informed me it was his first experience, and he agreed not to tell anyone I was getting married after graduation.

Many things were happening with the dispute with Mexico. So I penned another letter to Paw to bring him up to date.

1 May 1846

Dear Paw,

Polk has declared war on Mexico. The Mexican General Arista crossed the Rio Grande at Carricitios, and he engaged General Taylor at Palo Alto. Taylo's heavy artillery inflicted heavy losses on the Mexican army and sent them scampering back across the Rio Grande. We suffered a loss of about twenty men. The next day the Mexican army met us in a clash at Resaca de la Palma, and Taylor ran them all the way back to Matamoros. Taylor pursued Arista and conquered Matamoros.

Abraham Lincoln was the only congressman to oppose Polk on going to war with Mexico.

Polk's plan was for our western army to take California and New Mexico. Part of the army will seize northern Mexico, and another part will attack Mexico City. The navy will blockade the coast of Mexico, and it will later attack Tampico and Vera Cruz. I can hardly wait to become part of this operation. I know there will be lots of opportunities for an officer. My artillery training is going to be very beneficial in the war effort.

You know of my wedding plans, and I've made arrangements with John Singleton Mosby to stand up for me. I'll bring the bride home soon after the wedding. I may not have much time to spend considering Polk's war plans.

Give everyone my regards.

Your son,

Tom

Graduation day finally arrived, and a new dress officer uniform was issued to all graduating cadets. All were dressed in the new blue officer uniforms wearing white hats. By graduation I had increased my standing to seventeenth in the class. Custer remained at the bottom; however, he graduated. Who would ever guessed he would develop a record never to be broken in the army. He became the youngest officer to become a general. He was promoted to the rank of general at the age of twenty-two. Master Bates commented while giving me my commission that if I had another year I may have increased my class standing to number one. After graduation I had my first opportunity to stay at Mary's house in New York City. She, Rosemary and Stanfill attended the graduation exercises, and I return to their house after the reception.

We went directly to Mary's house at 400 Tenth Street. It was an older house with a smell as if it had been kept closed. It was evident the surrounding houses were constructed at the same time for one housing design had served the neighborhood. It contained running water, and there were two bedrooms upstairs with a kitchen and living room downstairs. Mary and I sat together in the living room while Rosemary served us tea. We discussed the wedding in detail.

The wedding was scheduled for two o'clock the next day. Mosby and Hiram stayed overnight for the occasion. Hiram had scheduled his return trip home on Sunday so he could attend the ceremony. I slept in the living room on a make-shift bed, and the next morning Rosemary served us breakfast as Stanfill hitched up the carriage to return to the Academy. I arrived at the barracks at eleven o'clock Saturday morning, and I met Mosby and Hiram in the barracks. We were dressed as second lieutenants in our new uniforms thirty minutes before the wedding. The big moment finally came, and the ceremony lasted fifteen minutes without flaws. Mosby kept Mary's wedding band clutched in his hand until the chaplain requested it. After the ceremony we went to Benny Havens Tavern for dinner. Mosby made a toast wishing us health and happiness, and Hiram drank, ate and drank some more.

After dinner we took Hiram and Mosby back to the barracks, and we bid each other farewell. We realized the opportunity would never present itself again to be together, as we had been at the Academy. I boarded the backseat of the carriage with Mary, and we embraced. I turned and waved to Hiram and John one last time. We returned to Mary's house, and we drank more of Rosemary's tea. Night came, and we were together with indescribable passion and lovemaking. The next day we made plans to travel to Clarksburg by train. The Academy had provided me with a return ticket home, and I was also instructed I would receive my orders to report for duty within the month.

Monday arrived, and Stanfill and Rosemary took us to the train station. We purchased a ticket to Clarksburg for Mary and boarded the train to arrive in Pittsburgh late Monday evening. There would be an overnight layover before the train completed the trip to Clarksburg. The train conductor recommended we stay at Mays Boarding House near the station. It was an adequate place serving dinner and breakfast for the cost of two dollars. After breakfast we boarded the train and continued our trip to Clarksburg. The family was there to meet the train. They were really interested in Mary and she them. Maw and Paw gave her a hug and the brothers and sisters followed, and she devoted herself to each one individually while getting acquainted. We loaded the buckboard and started home. Mary sat on the back with the girls allowing her feet dangle from the wagon. We were home within the hour, and Maw began to prepare dinner.

"Are you handy in the kitchen?" Maw asked.

"I know how to cook and clean."

"You can prepare the chicken then."

"Where is the icehouse?"

"We don't have an icehouse."

"Where do you keep the chickens?"

"In the chicken pen."

"Those are live chickens."

"Yes, they are."

"How am I supposed to prepare live chickens?"

"It's simple. I'll show you."

"First, you catch the chicken. Then, you tie its legs to a post with the chicken's head hanging down. After that, you cut its throat and allow the blood to drain. After the blood drains, you pluck the chicken feathers and singe away the pin-feathers. Now, you cut the chicken into parts and it's ready for frying."

"I never did this before. You have to kill the poor little chicken to eat it."

"I'm sure not going to eat a live one. You've never done this before? You'll learn, and you can have Tom do the catching, killing and singeing away the pin-feathers. He knows how. He's done this a plenty."

Maw gave Mary a cooking lesson she'd never forget. They performed their magic on each other at that cooking lesson and became friends. Anyone would like Mary for she had magic about her. It was more difficult for Mary to become acquainted with Paw. He was available at mealtime and in the evenings after milking the cows. Mary accompanied him milking on one occasion, and he play-fully squirted milk at her from the cow. She never tried the milking, and she was amazed at how large the hogs grew. Josh tried unsuccessfully to coax her into helping with the hog slopping. The family loved her.

During the next two weeks the family's hospitality welcomed Mary. Everyone had gotten to know everyone, and we were having a great visit until my instructions came from Washington to report to Fort Orleans. I would report to General Winfield Scott for engagement in the Mexican War, and I was excited. We started making plans for me to leave. Mary decided to remain another week with my folks before returning home. Along with my instructions was a train ticket from Clarksburg to New Orleans. It was a two-day travel. Monday came, and Mary and the family took me to the train station after breakfast. I boarded the train not realizing I would never see Mary again. It was a boring trip, and I napped often. I changed trains in Cincinnati the first day and spent the night in a sleeping berth. The next evening I arrived in New Orleans and went directly to the fort. I saluted the guard at the gate.

"I'm Second Lieutenant Thomas Jackson reporting for duty."

"Follow me, sir. I'll escort you to the general's office. He's awaiting your arrival."

I followed the private to the general's headquarters, and once inside his attaché invited me to have a seat. I seated myself in a rocking chair next to a window and explained to the attaché I was reporting for my first assignment under General Scott. The attaché explained the general was expecting me and would be available shortly. After a few minutes the general opened the door and announced to his attaché that he was ready to see me. The private motioned me inside the general office, and I saluted the general after entering.

"Welcome to Fort Orleans." Exclaimed Gen. Scott

"Thank you, sir."

"Did you have a good trip down here?"

"Yes sir."

"You must become familiar with the fort and New Orleans while you're here. Beware the French Quarters. A man can get in trouble there."

"I'll beware."

"We have a great task before us. We'll be leaving in two weeks with Admiral Bell and Colonel Braxton Braggs to enter the war from Mexico's East Coast. We'll be meeting Gen. Taylor in Mexico City or thereabouts one of these days. My attaché will show you to your quarters, and you will be issued uniforms tomorrow."

"Thank you, sir."

"Lieutenant, join me for dinner in the mess at six o'clock."

"Thank you, sir."

I was shown to my quarters. It was a small room in the corner of the fort. It was my first officers quarters. Unlike the Academy's barracks it was private. It still reminded me of my lonely days at the Academy, and it made me wonder where my fellow classmates were assigned. I settled into my new home and wrote a letter to Mary forwarding my new address. I met General Scott at dinner, and he introduced me to Colonel Braxton Braggs. I had already heard many stories about Colonel Braggs at the Academy. After dinner General Scott excused himself to join Mrs. Scott in their quarters. This gave Col. Braxton and me a chance to get acquainted. Braxton looked at me.

"Tom, let's get out of these dress uniforms and enjoy New Orleans."

"Sounds like a challenge to me, Colonel."

"I'll meet you here in fifteen minutes in civilian clothes."

Luckily I had kept my civilian clothes from home. I had learned from McClellan at the Academy how important civilian clothes were to an enlisted man. I was off to our meeting place inside the fort and Col. Braxton showed up shortly afterwards. The next thing I knew we were walking into New Orleans City limits. We stopped at the second bar and drank ale. By this time it was dark and the colonel was taking me to the French Quarters. We entered into a building with an arena containing an enclosed circular three-foot fence. When the building filled the roosters were brought to the center of the circular enclosure, an announcer appeared at the circular fence arena and announced the first cockfight.

"Place your bets, place your bets." He yelled.

Everyone started making bets on the two roosters being pitted. The roosters had been fitted with three-inch metal spurs placed over their natural spurs. Once the bets were in they let the cocks fight, and it was a gory affair. Finally, one rooster delivered a fatal blow, and the fight was over. The bet winners collected their money. Col. Braxton related that the opportunity to win the bet increased with the knowledge of the rooster's genealogy line. The winning rooster was a descendant of the Lawson Brown fighting cocks line. Col. Braxton really enjoyed watching the little birds fight to the death.

We returned to the fort and turned in. The next day we made preparation for our attack on Mexico by sea. The Academy never taught war preparation aboard a ship. We ordered cannon balls for the ship's cannons and for the eight and twelve pound land cannons. The ship's cannons were huge and fired non-exploding balls. The land cannons shot both exploding and non-exploding balls. Exploding balls were devastating for they were developed to annihilate advancing infantry. These balls could fan shrapnel for a ten-yard radius. Placed strategically three or four cannons could wipe out an advancing infantry. Gunpowder was shipped in kegs, and it was stored in airtight cargo holes in the ship. This was the last thing to be loaded onto the ship. It was loaded two weeks later, and we were ready to sail.

It was my first time to sail on the ocean. I had been so busy these past two week that I didn't have time to give any consideration to seasickness. Some of the soldiers succumb to the wicked nausea. However, it had no effect on me. I was focused on the job at hand. I received a letter from Mary before departing to learn she had returned home to Rosemary and Stanfill. She related how she enjoyed her visit in Clarksburg. She really enjoyed being with my folks. It was her first time to experience life in a big family. She related how she would miss the Saturday nights at Ben Havens Tavern this coming year, and how she was looking forward to my return.

We made efficient use of our sailing time by drilling and occasionally shooting the large cannons. We had been in the Gulf for two weeks now, and Gen. Scott summoned the officers to Admiral Bell's quarters for instructions.

He started, "Men, we've been at sea for two weeks now, and we're approaching our first target. We're two days from Tampico. We have three ships and three thousand troops. We must occupy Tampico before we can receive reinforcements. Braxton, I want you and Lt. Jackson to bombard the town until I can get troops ashore."

"Yes sir, if we align our three ships, we can alternately fire the ship cannons removing the town's wall and annihilate the army within. The Mexican cannons aren't large enough to deliver a blow to our ships." Braxton replied.

"I like a good advantage. Let's be on our way Adm. Bell."

"Consider it done."

Two days later we arrived off the coast of Tampico. The cannons were in place and the ships aligned. Gen. Scott gave the orders to begin firing, and we opened up to plan. The large ship's cannons rocked the ship with each shot. Infantry waded ashore to assault the city, and the walls around Tampico tumbled allowing an infantry attack. Col. Braggs taught me many artillery maneuvers during this attack. After the first hour of infantry engagement, the Mexican army was routed. We occupied the town by nightfall. We lost ten men with twenty others wounded, and there were two hundred and fifty Mexicans killed.

We searched the town to find the civilian population to be dispersed. We left a force of five hundred to defend the town and withdrew the ships to Lobo Island. Here, Gen. Scott ordered more supplies and requested more troops to further invasion efforts.

A week later five thousand additional troops and supplies arrived at Lobo Island.

CHAPTER 3

▼

THE MEXICAN WAR

The Mexican War began when Gen. Taylor crossed the Rio Nueces River and attacked the Mexican army in Palo Alto. The initial skirmish scattered the enemy. Days later he continued the attack when Gen. Arista's army was located again. He found his army outnumbered facing heavy Mexican artillery and musket fire. He ordered his men to lie down in the brush when he discovered his army was exposed. Once the Mexican cannons ceased firing his men charged through the brush skirmishing with the enemy. At day's end Taylor had taken Matamoros.

The American Navy had control of the Gulf of Mexico supplying Gen. Taylor with armaments, and Adm. Bell prevented Mexico from receiving shipments. At Lobo Island we treated our wounded, and Scott made plans for our next battle, Vera Cruz. We cleaned and prepared our ships, and Bell readied them for the next attack. Gen. Scott replenished our cannon balls, muskets and powder supplies. He also procured ten specially constructed boats for the infantry's shore attack when the invasion began. The beginning of the rainy season pressured us to begin out invasion. Gen. Scott assembled his staff in his tent.

"Gentlemen, Adm. Bell has informed me the ships are battle ready with invasion boats. These boats will carry the infantry ashore north of Vera Cruz, and we shall sail down to the fortification to start the initial attack. Any questions?"

No one uttered a sound.

"Col. Braggs, are your cannon ready for war?"

"Yes sir."

"Colonel, do you think our young Lt. Jackson is capable of commanding artillery in the follow-up ship?"

"Yes sir."

"Well, let's give him the opportunity and see what he can do. You'll be close enough to lend support."

"Lt. Jackson, you're in charge of the artillery on the follow-up ship. If there's a wall left standing at the Vera Cruz fortification you bring it down. Our sources indicate the Mexicans have Italian cannons on the walls and cliffs outside the city. Keep your eyes open. Any questions, anyone?"

Gen. Scott added, "One more thing, men. Gen. Quitmann will meet us in Vera Cruz when we arrive. His volunteer army with a new junior officer may join us for the battle once they secure the town of Alvarado."

I was really excited, and I wrote Paw a letter that evening to let the family know I was okay.

1847/March

Dear Paw,

I've been in my first Battle at Tampico. It was a great experience. We bombarded the city with cannon fire early one morning for about an hour taking out their artillery and all fortifications. My artillery training at the Academy really served me well. Many cannon shots were on target based on the calculations I learned in my Natural Philosophy classes. Col. Braggs taught me how to bring down the fortification walls using the larger ships cannons. Water absorbs the cannons' percussion creating waves from these cannons. We're continuing our invasion of Mexico from the east coast, and our plans are to meet Gen. Taylor in Mexico City.

Give the family my love, and tell them I miss them.

Your son,

Tom

I finished the letter in time to receive a letter from Mary. The letter related that she was living with Rosemary and Stanfill, and she had planted a flower garden near their back porch. Maw had taught her to plant flowers while she was in

Clarksburg. She had visited the doctor to be diagnosed with depression, and she indicated she would require money for medication. I immediately sent her thirty-five dollars from the forty-three per month I received for Second Lieutenant pay.

The next day we rolled out at daylight maneuvering into position for battle. I was in the follow-up ship loading the ship's cannon. The infantry disembarked at the designated invasion point, and we sailed within cannon range of Vera Cruz. The lead ship's cannon opened fire on the fortification walls removing the cannons. The Mexican fortification returned fire with cannon balls falling a hundred yards short of the ship. Adm. Bell changed directions of the lead ship moving it further from Vera Cruz. The other ships absorbed the percussion waves, and they moved into place taking their shots. Finally, the follow up ship was in place to make her approach, and a hidden Mexican cannon fired from a cliff. The ball was off mark by forty yards.

"Sergeant Johnson, aim two of your cannon at the cliff. Aim one at the cannon, and the other above the cannon on the cliff."

"Yes sir." He replied as he quickly surveyed the cannon location. Sergeant Johnson was a good artilleryman, a well-trained soldier who learned to fire artillery on the job.

"Fire when you're ready, Sergeant."

An instant later Sergeant Johnson fired, and his first charge was slightly below the Mexican cannon jarring the cliff. However, the second shot brought down the rock wall above the cannon. The Mexicans manning the cannons jumped to their deaths on the rocks below, and I proceeded by the remaining fortifying walls delivering my deadly parcels. We sailed in this pattern for the remainder of the day. Gen. Scott sent a messenger to the follow-up boat requesting me to take an eight-pound cannon to land. Once ashore I was to assemble the cannon and attack the castle of San Juan d'Ulloa. I immediately disassembled the cannon, and placed it in the landing boat. Once on land I reassembled the cannon with the help of the infantrymen meeting me. They brought army mules and wagons to pull the cannon and haul munitions. When we arrived at the castle I placed the cannon in firing position with load. Gen. Scott and Adm. Bell continued their bombardment from sea. The infantry was in place, and I began firing the eight-pounder. My second shot fragmented the castle gate. The infantry was already firing and advancing toward the castle, and I continued to fire taking out the corner enclosed musket positions. Finally, the castle capitulated, and I was reloading when someone spoke from behind.

"Okay, Tom. You can quit now. They've given up."

It was Hiram. He pulled a flask from his pocket and said, "Have a drink."

"Thanks, Hiram. I believe I will. It's good to see you. How did you get here?"

"Well, it's a long story. Gen. Taylor sent me along with Gen. Quitmann to help with these volunteers. They're good men but no military training."

"It's good to see you anyway."

"Tom, let's move into the castle and review the spoils."

The next day Col. Braggs and I were summoned to Gen. Scott's quarters. He proceeded to tell us what a good job we had done. Braxton was promoted to Lieutenant General, and I was promoted to a full Lieutenant. Hiram and I spent the day investigating the ruins of Vera Cruz and the castle. Hiram located a little cantina where we sampled the only liquor left in Vera Cruz, and we remained there until evening. The next day we arrived at the cantina earlier. Mexican senioritis joined us after we supplied them a couple rounds of Mexican beer, and they told us how they were treated by the Creoles, who traced family origins to Spain. The Creoles were the wealthy Mexicans, who were served by landless peasants, Mestizos or Indians. The Mestizos senioritis were olive skinned beauties. Their black hair with a blue hue flowed down their backs. These girls became more romantic in proportion to the amount of beer they drank. Hiram really enjoyed this part of Mexico, and I grew used to it as the evening progressed. After four hours in the cantina I was still able to find my way to my quarters, and I left Hiram there. The next day I met him for dinner.

"Tom, let's get some dinner. I haven't eaten since yesterday. I spent last night in the cantina, and someone took all my money. Can I borrow two dollars until next Saturday, payday? It seems as if I'm still borrowing money from you the same way when we were at the Academy."

"Sure, Hiram. You noticed that. Here's two dollars. It's war time, and money doesn't mean much to us now anyway." Hiram didn't know that all I had in my pocket was ten dollars. Mary had made a big demand on my monthly pay so she could get medicine for her depression ailment.

We continued to occupy and assess the damage at Vera Cruz. Gen. Scott withdrew his main forces to Lobo Island to make plans for further attacks. He left a small force within the city to maintain our presence, and Hiram and I didn't mind the assignment. We stayed in Vera Cruz three more weeks, and a courier finally delivered the mail and our monthly pay. Hiram repaid me the two dollars. I had another letter from Mary, and she was requesting more money for medication. She expressed the pain and suffering from her ailment. Again I sent her half my monthly pay, and at this rate I may be borrowing money from Hiram before the month was over. We spent the rest of the week there, and as far as Hiram and

I were concerned we could've stayed longer. I managed to get Hiram to his quarters every night so he didn't sleep in the cantina. He had taken to enjoying the Mestizos girls. At weeks end a courier brought our orders from Gen. Scott. We would be joining the main body of the army marching on Santa Anna in Jalapa, Mexico.

The march would be a two-day affair for Jalapa was fifteen miles from Verz Cruz through mountainous terrain. Gen. Scott would leave a small garrison behind to maintain the city. I pulled Hiram away kicking and screaming, and I had never seen anyone wanting to stay in a ruined devastated city so much.

It was April 1847, and we had pursued Santa Anna to the mountain of Cerro Gordo on the road to Jalapa. He had constructed barricades at the Rio del Plan and on the road to Jalapa. He had lethal firing power with their cannons and muskets in position; however, the Mexican soldier fired his muskets mainly from the hip usually shooting over the heads of our advancing infantry. He had to load the musket with extra powder to achieve the same affect as our muskets, and their muskets carried a harder kick when fired. We routed Santa Anna's army by fighting our way up the mountain. The dead Mexicans strewed the mountainside, and I had become so accustomed to the wounded and dead bodies didn't bother me anymore. The dead bodies were like a hog ready to be butchered. I always knew that one day I would be subjected to such a scene, and I accepted that fact. We walked over the dead leaving them for the buzzards or their countrymen to bury.

We tended our wounded and returned them to the ship's doctor. Eight more American soldiers died in battle, and we buried our dead and marched onto Jalapa. The next day we marched into Jalapa unopposed, and we performed a military house to house search for the enemy. The town was unoccupied so we made camp. Gen. Scott ordered Hiram and me to escort the volunteer army to Vera Cruz then onto New Orleans where they would be mustered out of service. We spent most of the night before leaving Vera Cruz in the cantina enjoying the Mexican beer and beauties. We got in enough sleeping time to make us presentable for the voyage to New Orleans the next day. The voyage took three days, and I was sick vomiting over the side of the ship the first day. Hiram vomited all three days, and he quit when his feet were on land again. Hiram even swore off drinking until he was on land.

The volunteers mustered out, and Hiram and I were off to see the cock fights in the French Quarters. Hiram wasn't too impressed with the chicken fights, but he really liked the nightlife in New Orleans. He was himself again in the French Quarters saloons with no thoughts of his recent sickness. After two days we were given our orders to join Gen. Taylor in Matamoros. Hiram had been made Gen. Taylor's quartermaster, and I had been put in command of the artillery. I had grown very fond of Braxton's ship cannon, and I recognized the opportunity to get the artillery I needed for future campaigns. I told Hiram to order me two ship's cannons with exploding cannon balls loaded with nails. Hiram thought my request was unusual, but he decided to go along once I explained my plan. The supplies were there within a week, and I drilled with Gen. Taylor's artillery squad. In the evenings Hiram and I managed to locate a good saloon. We missed the Meszitos senioritis of Vera Cruz, but we made do with the Indian girls of Matamoros. I said my goodbye to Hiram in the saloon on Friday night.

The next morning I harnessed the two large cannons to four army mules the way I used to harness Samantha to plow. The army mules were strong; however, pulling those cannons was still a difficult task for them. The specially prepared exploding cannon balls were loaded onto wagons in crates. There were three tons of these balls. Each wagon had one ton of cannon balls, and was pulled by a team of four army mules. We begin our march to Monterey. The march was difficult for the young soldiers. It was difficult for them to adjust to the heat, cactus, dessert, disease and sagebrush. They were new recruits and had enlisted under a congressional declaration. The congressional declaration had established the length of time new recruits served, and most recruits enlisted for a tour of duty lasting twelve months. It was a boring march with the heat endurance, boredom and insects. Battle was the only thing these soldiers had to look forward to. Maybe they could spend time with Mexican senioritis and drink warm beer. These young men came to serve their country's cause and save Texas. They were there to carry the burden and hardship of freeing Texas from Mexican aggression. They came to avenge Santa Anna's aggressive action.

A courier overtook us with news of other forces encamped throughout Mexico. News from Camargo, on the banks of the San Juan River, related that disease was killing more Americans than bullets. I visited there in my present state to find the news to be true. New troops had not been taught the methods to keep camping quarters in sanitary conditions. The same source of water was used for drinking, cooking and bathing causing illness to run rampant through camps. Dysentery, measles and other ailments were widespread taking many new recruits to early graves. Treatment methods for these diseases were nonexistent in the primitive surroundings.

We arrived at Gen. Taylor's headquarters a week later, and I was issued a new forage cap and a revolver side arm. I had never worn a side arm before; however, I grew use to it. If the little devils broke through the lines near my cannon I needed a weapon for close encounters. I could shoot as accurately with a sidearm as I could with a cannon. Taylor's army was made up of Texas volunteers and Mississippi regular. The Texans wore all types of uniforms from buckskins to regular issue. The Mississippi regulars wore straw hats and were commanded by Col. Jefferson Davis. The Texans were always armed with knives, pistols and revolvers, and they carried weapons in their boots, belts and shirts. The Mississippians were regular army except for the hats. We marched for five days to arrive within three miles of Monterey and made camp. We met in Gen.Taylor's tent to prepare battle plans the first evening. Taylor knew the battle would be fought in the open with only sagebrush for cover, and he carefully laid out his battle plans. I remained behind to discuss the artillery involvement.

"Gen. Taylor, I wish to speak with you, sir."

"Why sure, Lt. Jackson. How can I help you?"

"I wish to modify your plans for artillery support during the battle."

"Let's hear your plan, Lieutenant."

"Sir, I have dragged large ship cannons and special charged exploding cannon balls from Matamoros to use in this battle. I plan to mount the cannons on regular cannon mounts anchoring them in front with chains. I can reduce the charge to minimize the cannon percussion, and if the cannons move backward too much I can reposition them with mules. The cannon balls are loaded with nails, and I expect to kill from fifty to one hundred Mexican infantrymen with each shot."

"It's worth trying, Lieutenant. Especially since you've gone to all the trouble to drag 'em cannons here. I see you've already put a great deal of planning into your operation, and I'd like to hear the rest of your plan."

"I would like to position the cannons in the front lines with the infantry. When the battle begins I will fire the cannons alternately with the infantry, and this will allow me time to reload."

"Lieutenant, it sounds like a good plan to me. We'll prepare for battle tomorrow."

We posted sentries, and I went to my quarters for a restless night. The next day we advanced toward Monterey positioning ourselves for battle. Our scouts reported the Mexicans were advancing to meet us. We located a knoll about a half-mile from Monterey for the battle line, and I positioned my cannons on the front line with the infantry. The eight and twelve pound cannons were strategically placed in accordance to regular battle plans. We could see the Mexican army advancing now to within five hundred yards. I gave the command for the two large cannons to fire simultaneously.

"Fire!"

The two shots took out three hundred Mexican infantrymen, and the front line of the Mexican infantry scattered. Our infantry begin firing.

"Reload and reposition the cannons by ten degrees."

The cannons' percussion wasn't as great as I had anticipated. The charge wasn't great enough to move the heavy guns significantly. I surveyed the Mexican advancement and repositioned the cannons. I commanded again.

"Fire!"

Again, the cannon fire removed another three to four hundred Mexicans, and they started to retreat. I could see the Mexican officers urging them into battle. The officers were slashing at their infantrymen with their swords urging them back into battle, and now it became a game. We would reload, and when the Mexican army advanced our infantry and my two big cannons were efficient. The Mexican army made four advances before retreating, and the four advances cost them three thousand men. Our losses were three dead infantrymen and two army mules. After the firing subsided we advanced onto the battleground to review the remains. The Mexican soldiers were impaled with nails and scrapple, and Mexican dead littered the ground. They retreated fast leaving their dead and wounded. We continued to advance onto Monterey, and we occupied the city without further resistance. The remaining Mexican army retreated toward Mexico City, and we secured Monterey and made camp.

Gen. Taylor summoned me to his quarters. I entered and saluted.

"Lieutenant, that was a classic maneuver. I am empowered under special circumstances to make battlefield promotions, and I think your performance today warrants a special circumstance. Tom, your performance today has earned you a promotion to captain."

"Thank you, sir." I saluted.

"Captain, if you have anymore battlefield plans similar to the one you used today feel free to employ them."

"Thank you, sir." I saluted again and was dismissed.

I headed straight to the saloon in the middle of Monterey. It was well stocked with warm Mexican beer, and I had a well-deserved one. After I finished my beer I returned to find my quarters. Once inside, the events of the day collapsed on me. I stood on my ahead against the wall for ten minutes to redistribute my blood. The exercise made me feel really good, and then I rested on my bed. The next thing I realized it was morning. We breakfasted at an inn, which had been converted into army quarters. The coffee was fresh, and someone had commandeered local fresh eggs. We also had lemons, oranges and grapefruit, and I stuck three lemons in my pocket for later in the day.

A courier had overtaken us with the news and the mail. I had a letter from Mary, and she related that Rosemary, Stanfill and she had moved to a location on Church Street in New York City. She needed more money to replenish her medication. I had not received more pay, and I only had five dollars. I sent it to her.

After securing Monterey we waited for supplies. Hiram sent me a box of lemons with the munitions. He hadn't forgotten my appetite for citrus. He also included three more ton of cannon balls for my new cannons. He added a note that these cannon balls were loaded with undersize minie balls, .037 calibre. Exploding cannon balls containing minie balls were better than shooting the enemy with my revolver. We were quite settled at Monterey awaiting orders from Polk, and Polk was waiting to see what Gen. Scott's next actions were. In August, Gen. Scott advanced his forces toward Mexico City. His army beat back Santa Anna forcing his to retreat to Mexico City, and he fortified the city for the siege. He had recuperated from the Battle of Cerro Gordo losses. Scott surrounded Mexico City without advancing on it, and he entertained hopes of preventing further bloodshed. He chose to allow diplomacy to prevail.

We were beginning to make Monterey our home, and Hiram kept sending the lemons. Once he included a bottle of Tennessee sipping whiskey. He must to have had an extra case to allow a bottle to get away. I had received two more letters from Mary requesting more money for medication, and each letter was more desperate than the one before. I was sending the money at a controlled pace so she wouldn't spend it all at one time. She always agonized with the pain in her letters, and she related that Rosemary and Stanfill comforted her. I often wished I could be at her side.

Santa Anna negotiated with Nicholas Trist, the American ambassador, into mid-September to buy himself extra time. At this time it was determined the negotiations had failed, and we were ordered to march south on Mexico City. When we arrived, Gen. Scott had already made preparation to attack the City starting at Molino del Rey. Molino del Rey joined Mexico City to the south, and Taylor's army was to assist by attacking the fortress of Chapultepec. Gen. Taylor summoned me to his quarters prior to the attack.

"What's your input on attacking this fort, Tom?"

After studying the maps and terrain I replied, "Sir, I would like to employ the method used at Vera Cruz to enter the fort. I can blow down the fort gate and front wall with regular cannon balls fired from my large cannons. We definitely will need to anchor the cannons for the percussion. In fact, after we fire the cannons we may not be able to use them again."

"That's okay. If they get us within the stucco fort walls they will have done their jobs. Have the men prepare the anchors for those cannons."

"Yes sir." I saluted and left.

We anchored the cannons at five hundred yards from the fort gates. Gen. Scott had arrived with his forces after defeating the Mexican in a short battle at Molino del Rey. Our army was in place, and my plan was to fire the cannons simultaneously at the gate and wall. The attack was ordered by Scott, and I cleared everyone from the cannon area. The sergeant set off the charges. The gates and entire north wall collapsed, and the anchors held the cannons in place. However, they did rise like a bucking horse. I reloaded and fired again removing the surrounding buildings on each side.

The Mexican army was returning our fire now so my cannon crew continued firing the exploding cannon balls. A few cannon shots enabled our troops to enter the city almost unopposed. The marines passed thousands of the Mexican army dead from the cannon shots, and they continued fighting their way to the Main Plaza and the National Palace, the Halls of Montezumas. The marines raised the American flag at the top of Mexico's National Palace. Santa Anna's forces fled Mexico City in disarray. Gen. Scott summoned me to his quarters within Mexico City.

"Captain Jackson, that was a fine piece of work you did in clearing the fort gate and wall. Your cannon techniques allowed us to enter the fort with little resistance, and at this time I would like to address you with another battlefield promotion to the rank of Major."

"Thank you, sir" I saluted.

"Thank you, Major." He returned my salute.

It was late in the afternoon I headed straight for the saloon in the Main Plaza. It was already filled with soldiers celebrating victory, and the Mexican beer flowed freely. I returned to my quarters late that evening only to awake the next day with a throbbing headache. We continued to celebrate all week, and the young Indian girls started returning to the saloon making the celebration all the more enjoyable.

Once again Trist discussed a treaty with Mexico. He proposed Mexico concede the right to annex Texas, fixing the boundaries at the Rio Grande and the concession of New Mexico with the upper and lower territory of California. The treaty agreement dragged on for months with Polk growing more impatient with

Mexican cooperation. In late January the treaty was approaching being signed. Trist and Mexican leaders, Couto, Atristan and Cuevas finally came to an agreement. Mexico agreed to all concessions except Lower California, and we would pay fifteen million dollars for Upper California.

Gen. Scott ordered me to return to Matamoros as the commanding officer of the troops remaining there, and Hiram had been recalled to Fort Orleans. He shipped me the supplies, and I dispersed them to the army in Mexico City. I recalled our favorite saloons in Matamoros and frequented them often.

A courier arrived at my quarters with a special delivery letter from Rosemary Morrison. I knew it couldn't be good news, and it began with Rosemary relating that Mary had succumbed to an overdose of her medication. She had been taking laudanum for her ailment, and she had been buried in a local cemetery three days earlier. I continued to read the letter, but the remainder was meaningless. We had almost four wonderful weeks together, and now she was gone. I immediately penned a letter to my superiors relating my circumstances, and their response was favorable. I would be released as soon as my replacement arrived, and the replacement was dispatched immediately. He showed up two week later armed to the teeth with pistols, revolvers, knives, ammunition belts and two sabers. It was amazing he didn't hurt himself. I was sitting at the table with my back to the door when he came in.

"Second Lieutenant reporting for duty."

I turned around and saluted him to see the astonishment on his face. "It about time you got here, Ambrose. Where have you been the past two weeks?"

"Tom, it's you. You've become a major already. No one told me who I would be replacing, and that there was a need to rush. I've been in New Orleans and Monterey partying, and the women in New Orleans wouldn't let me leave. I picked up all this armament at Fort Orleans."

"Yes, there was a rush to get you here. My wife died in New York City about three weeks ago. She took too much medication, laudanum, and she had a negative response to it. I got a letter from her mother, Rosemary, describing her demise."

"I'm sorry to hear about that, Tom. Where did she live in New York? I really liked that girl."

"She lived at 400 Church Street with her parents at the time of her death."

"Tom, do you know what formally was located at that address?"

"No, tell me."

"Tom, Rosie's house of ill-repute was located there. I was there my first year at the Academy. It was where I contacted gonorrhea, which turned into prostatitis. It still plagues me today."

"Are you sure?"

"Yes. I'm very sorry about Mary. She was a sweet fun-loving girl."

"She was. Yes, she was. It's dinnertime Ambrose. Let get some dinner, and I'll show you the town. We'll reminisce our days at the Academy."

"Sounds good to me, Major."

"It's okay. Just call me Tom."

"Okay, Tom. Would you call me Hill or A.P.? Call me anything but Ambrose. You've been calling me Ambrose all the years we were at the Academy. It kills me. Ambrose? What kind of name is that for a man of my caliber?"

Tom laughed, "Okay, A.P., I'll do my best but don't piss me off." We laughed like we did when he returned to the Academy after being away with his ailment.

"A.P., you won't believe who my quarter master is at Fort Orleans. It's Hiram Simpson Grant, and he and I have been together over half of Mexico. He's a damn great soldier when he's not drunk, and he likes the Mexican senioritis."

"Well, Tom. I had some fun with those senioritis myself in Monterey. I think I fall in love every time I see those big breasts, olive skin, shinny black hair and tiny waistlines, and I minimized falling in love to three times an evening."

"A.P., you haven't changed since you were at the Academy." We arrived at the Inn for dinner. We were having a ham dinner, which reminded me of home.

"Tell me, Hill. Did you enjoy your last year at the Academy?"

"Like you wouldn't believe. You know I shared a room with Hull, and our room became known as Hotel West Point. The ladies from Benny Havens Tavern slipped into our room almost every night. You know they hardly gave upper classmen demerits, and Hull and I got our limit. We were caught three times with ladies in our beds. They would have given Lee demerits for that."

"A.P., I'm going to take you to the saloon on the Main Plaza here in Mexico City. The young Indian girls are frequenting the place again. After we took the city only the soldiers hung out in this saloon. I can't promise you anything exciting, but after tonight you're on your own. Tomorrow I'll be on my way to New Orleans, then onto New York City."

"I'll see you to the boat in the morning, Tom."

I woke A.P. early, and we had breakfast. After breakfast we walked down to the dock to a boat which took me to the ship. A.P. turned to me.

"Tom, it was good to see you again. Tell me something. Do you know what laudanum is?"

"It was the medication Mary was taking for her depression."

"Tom, laudanum is an opium laced drink. The Chinese uses it for medication and to get high, and it does things to them what liquor does to us only to a greater extent. It makes one feel no pain."

"What are you telling me, A.P.?"

"I'm not exactly sure, Tom. I only know things I've heard about laudanum. I never knew anyone who took the stuff for medicine or otherwise. The only thing I know is that it's not a good thing to take."

"Well, I'm glad you told me. I'll look into it when I get to New York. It's good to see you again, and I'll tell Hiram you replaced me here. Good luck."

"Good luck to you, Tom. I hope you get things straightened out about Mary. Again, I'm very sorry for you."

I boarded the boat taking me to the ship, and as it left the dock I turned and waved goodbye to A.P. once again. Shortly, I was boarding the ship for my return trip to New Orleans, and it was a four-day boring trip. We finally arrived early Friday morning. I went straight to Fort Orleans and checked in with the Colonel. His orderly found me quarters, and I dropped off my gear and went looking for Hiram.

I found him in the back of the commissary checking in supplies. "What ya doing, Hiram?"

Without looking he replied, "Checking in supplies."

"Lieutenant, don't you salute a superior officer anymore?" He immediately turned and saluted.

"Tom, how did you become a major? It's good to see you again. I've been stuck here issuing supplies while you're warring with the Mexicans."

"I became a major by fighting the Mexicans. I was in six major battles including the invasion of Mexico City. It was your help, which made me successful. You got me the cannons and exploding cannon balls. Those exploding balls wiped out those Mexicans."

"You'll have to tell me all about it at dinner and later tonight when we go looking for some Creole ladies. What brings you to New Orleans?"

"I'll bring you up to date, Hiram. But would you do me a favor first?"

"What's that, Tom?"

"Would you salute me one more time?"

"Get out of here, Tom." He laughed.

"First, A.P. was my replacement in Mexico. I waited two weeks for him to get there. He wanted in the war so badly that he went chasing bandits for some action causing him to be late. When he arrived, he was loaded with guns and knives. He had revolvers and pistols in holsters, gun belts and his boots. If he were to stumble and fall, he would have either shot or cut himself. He sends his regards."

"Well, I guess if you enjoyed seeing him I'd like to see him too."

"The main reason I'm here is I must returning to New York. My wife died three weeks ago. She was suffering from depression, and she had a negative reaction to her medicine."

"Tom, I'm sorry to hear about Mary. She was really a fun girl when we were at the Academy."

"Thanks, Hiram. I'm leaving on the train tomorrow morning."

"That leaves us dinner and the evening together."

We were off to the fort's mess hall, and it was good Creole cooking for a change. Hiram and I ate well, and we went directly to New Orleans after dinner. We attended Hiram's frequent hangouts near the cock-fighting arena. We never had time for the Creole ladies for Hiram was having a heavy drinking evening. We reminisced about the days at the Academy, and I concluded the evening before he became too intoxicated. We finally arrived at Hiram's quarters, and he enticed me to sleep on a cot in his quarters. As we went to bed I called to Grant.

"Hiram."

"What?"

"Would you salute me one more time."

"Get outa here, Tom."

We turned in. Later, Hiram woke me.

"Tom, do you still want me to salute you?"

"No. Go to sleep. I have to catch the train in the morning."

"Just checking."

Morning came soon, and Hiram had recovered enough for breakfast, and he walked with me to the train station. The train was waiting, and I retrieved my ticket from my pocket and turned toward Hiram.

"You know something Hiram?"

"What?"

"You don't have to salute me anymore."

We said our good-byes, and I boarded the train. I sat next to the window and opened it. Hiram was still standing there, and I waved to him as the train pulled away from the station. I didn't realize it, but I would never see Hiram again. He would quit drinking and rise through the ranks to become a great general. He was always good at war strategy at the Academy. I arrived at the Academy after four days traveling and met with the commandant. He supplied me quarters, and we discussed my current rank. I told him about my participation in the Mexican War, and he told me he wasn't surprised at my promotions. He related how my drive to succeed at the Academy aided me in accomplishing my goal. We talked at length, and I explained my return to the Academy. He allowed me to use the Academy's quarters until I had my affairs in order, and I was also allowed to use Little Sorrell to travel around the city.

I left the Academy after breakfast the following day. I rode Little Sorrell all day, often stopping to ask directions to Church Street. Each time I asked someone, the asking was met with laughs and snickers. I arrived at 400 Church Street late that evening. It was an unusual business establishment with the name Rosie over the door. I tied Little Sorrell at the hitching post and knocked on the door. A well-dressed young lady opened the door.

"Well hello, General. Who do we have here?"

"I'm not a general. I am Major Thomas Jackson, and I'm here to see Rosemary and Stanfill Morrison."

"You're Mary's husband. We really miss Mary. She was such a good person. It was laudanum, you know."

"Yes, I know. Would you summon the Morrisons please."

"Why yes, sweetheart. You just wait here."

"Rebecca, do you know where Rosie and the Colonel are?"

"Rosie is upstairs and the Colonel is cleaning out the trash bin. We've been after that lazy bum all day to clean it. I'll get Rosie for you."

She moved to the stairs and yelled, "Rosie, you have a client down here. This one's a looker, and if you don't come down I'm going to take care of him."

Rosemary appeared at the top of the stairs dressed in a housecoat. She didn't see me until she was half way down the stairs. Surprised she said, "Now Tom, I can explain." She turned to Rebecca, "Would you have Stanfill come inside. We have a guest."

Rebecca went for Stanfill immediately, and he came through the door to see Rosemary and me in the sitting room. He started, "They made me do it. I'm just help around here. They call me the colonel making fun of me. I'm not a real colonel, and I'm not Mary's father and Rosemary isn't Mary's mother."

"Sit down and shut up, Stanfill." Rosemary ordered.

Stanfill immediately took a chair.

Rosemary began, "I suppose you're here to find out about Mary."

"Yes, I am."

"Well, it's a long story about Mary. Where do you want me to begin?"

"How about in the beginning."

"Well, Mary came here when she was about nine years old. She just showed up at the door one day. She was a runaway, and she would never tell us who her parents were. We gave her a place to stay and fed her, and she paid her keep by doing odd jobs for the girls. We kept her sheltered as much as we could from our business activities here at the house. She learned though as she got older, and we had to work even harder keeping her on the right track. Our carriage took her to Ben Havens Tavern ever Saturday night when you were at the Academy for Saturday night was our busiest time. Sending her out was successful for about a year then I got sick, and she had to care for me. That was what she was doing until you married her. She returned back here from Clarksburg after you went off to war. We stayed at the house on Tenth Street until the lease expired then we moved back here. Once there was a chance for her to marry a West Point cadet, we planned the entire affair with me being her mother and Stanfill her father. After she came back from Clarksburg, she roomed with a girl upstairs. The girl had been taking laudanum all the time we had known her, and she gave the laudanum to Mary. Mary developed a craving for it, and she bought laudanum with the money you sent. Four weeks ago she didn't come to breakfast, and we checked to find her dead in bed. I don't know what else to say."

"Well, I don't know what to say either. I loved that girl. We were together such a short time. I had so many plans for us, and I don't know what I'll do now."

"You can start by spending the night here. We have a guest bedroom upstairs. I know you had a hard day."

"I was only trying to help out." Stanfill confessed.

"I know, Stanfill. Don't worry about it. Show me to my room."

"Sure, General."

"I'm a major, not a general. And I'm a real major."

"How'd you get to be a major?"

"It was the Mexican War, and there were battlefield promotions. I was promoted to a major."

Stanfill retrieved my bag from Little Sorrell, and he led the way to my bedroom. He returned to put Little Sorrell in the stable behind the house. I was tired, and after washing my face in the basin I went to bed. It was a restless sleep I had that night. Rosemary woke me at breakfast, and she apologized again and again about the scenario they created to trap me for Mary. I finally admitted not minding being trapped by Mary for the times with her were the happiest days of my life. I left Rosie's after breakfast never to see Rosemary or Stanfill again in my mortal state. As I rode back to the Academy I stopped by the cemetery to visit her grave. I said my goodbye to her, and I recalled our many good times together especially those we shared at Ben Havens Tavern. She could make me feel so good. She had left a void in my life, and it would take some time for me to heal.

I arrived at the Academy sooner than I expected. I knew the way back and didn't have to ask directions. I curried and stabled Little Sorrell. She had been a faithful horse. I walked around the Academy and down to the river, and I sat at the river recalling the good times with Mary. I returned to my quarters in time for evening dinner. I didn't realize it, but it was Saturday night and the cadets were getting ready for Benny Havens Tavern. I returned to my quarters and prepared to go with them for old time sake. The young cadets raced ahead by the farm to the Tavern, and I recalled the goat escapade on the way. I entered Ben Havens to be recognized by Mr. Havens. We exchanged pleasantries and I related my promotions to major. The cadets and girls were young, and I wondered if there was a Mary among them. I visited the billiards room and the poker room, but it wasn't the same. The music was the same, and I could see cadets there similar to the ones when I was in school. Unable to endure the loneliness I returned to the Academy early. I remained at the Academy three more days to instruct the cadets on the new cannon techniques. The last day I visited Little Sorrell at the stable and curried her one last time.

The next day I boarded the train for Clarksburg. It was the usual two-day trip, and these two days gave me time to mourn Mary. I recalled every time we were together, and how she enjoyed the dancing and the passion behind Ben Havens Tavern. The longest time we spent together was the time in Clarksburg with my family. I arrived in Clarksburg and decided to walk to the farm. As I arrived at the entrance to the farm, I looked up the dirt road to see the family sitting on the porch. I started up the road to find the family had spotted me, and they rushed to meet me. We spent the entire afternoon on that front porch. After dinner I told them all about the war, and they were intrigued and happy I returned unharmed. I explained all about the cannons and my promotions again and again. At evening's end Paw and I walked to the barn.

"Tom, is there anything you want to talk about concerning Mary?"

"No, Paw. I loved her. She was sick and the medicine killed her. She really enjoyed visiting here with you and the family."

"We enjoyed her. She grew on everyone. We loved her too."

"Paw, what did you do with the hogs?"

"We ate 'em. The tobacco base is doing so well I decided not to raise hogs anymore. It's easy to buy ham and bacon with the tobacco money."

"I bet you broke Josh's heart. No more feedings."

"He works hard putting the tobacco up in the barn every year. It's cleaner work though. Let's go back to the house. I just wanted to talk to you alone. You know you can always talk to me about personal matters. Tell me about the treaty."

"Sure, Paw." We started back toward the house.

"I wrote you about some of the treaty details, and how we expected a peace treaty would be negotiated soon. Initially, Polk sent Trist to make our treaty proposals to Santa Anna, and he rejected the offer. Santa Anna's downfall came shortly after this rejection. The Mexican people were tired of living in war turmoil, and Mexico was without a leader. Manuel Pena was instated as the new Minister of Mexico, and Trist again presented the treaty to the new Mexican minister in Guadalupe Hidalgo. We demanded Mexico to concede New Mexico, Upper and Lower California, and the right for Texas to become part of the United States. Pena agreed to all terms of the treaty except two. Mexico wanted to keep Lower California, and he wanted to be paid fifteen million dollars for other concessions. In January 1848, Mexico and the United States signed the Treaty of Guadalupe Hidalgo, and it was ratified later when congress approved it."

"Well, I glad to see us get some land out of the war. I don't understand why we have to pay for it."

"It's the right thing to do. The people in the areas have accrued debt with the Mexican government, and the money will settle the debt."

The next two weeks I told and retold Mexican War battles, and my orders finally arrived to report to Fort Carroll. I left two days later to assume duties serving under Lieutenant Colonel Robert E. Lee. Here, we became good friends for Lee was a true leader. However, duties at Fort Carroll were routine and boring, and I missed the war. It was my calling, and I was good at waging war.

In December 1850, I returned to Clarksburg to visit family for a month. It was my annual furlough, and I was looking forward to spending it with family. The second day I was there Maw invited Elinor Junkins for a visit. It was Maw's way to look out for me. Elinor and I became reacquainted spending the entire furlough together every evening, and she never mentioned my marriage to Mary. We were married Christmas Eve, and we returned to the fort shortly afterwards. Her brothers did not want her to leave home; however, she explained to them that they must learn to take care of themselves or find wives.

We were assigned married officer's quarters, and Elinor adapted to army life in the fort. The weekends were spent horseback riding through the countryside, and she became involved in activities with other officers' wives. Elinor removed the atmosphere of daily boring drills. I raced to our quarters every evening to spend the evening in front of the fireplace with her.

In 1851, I procured a teaching position at Virginia Military Institute. I taught Natural Philosophy and Artillery to the cadets. It was a major change in our life style, and I resigned the army. We started family planning, and I began teaching. At first, the cadets were overwhelmed having me as a teacher. The stories of my battlefield promotions had made national news, and they had been circulated at the academies. I didn't realize civilians still remembered me as a hero from the Mexican War. Beginning the first day I had to tell about the Mexican War battles, and it seemed as if the cadets couldn't get enough of these war stories. The second day it became obvious the cadets were using my war stories as a means to get away from the Natural Philosophy studies. I put a halt to that by requiring them to quote the problems and the pages they came from. When they asked me a problem, I quoted the page it came from and the page the solution came from. At the end of class the third day young John Holden became inquisitive.

"Why do you always eat lemons and hold one arm in the air?"

"Well, John. I eat lemons because I like them, and I hold my arms in the air to redistribute the blood in my body. I have other exercises for the same purpose. I stand on my head ten minutes every evening before bedtime. You should try it sometimes."

These cadets had no trouble with square root or any other mathematical problems, and they required little tutoring. I held them to learning the Natural Philosophy's lessons, and they developed names for me like Tom Fool and Old Jack. My devotion to discipline and rules kept the cadets on their toes, and in turn it made me a mark for the cadets' mischief. I tolerated their mischief to get them educated. The third month at VMI I was on the way to class via the Institute Building when a brick dropped at my feet. I looked up to find Henry Wadsworth leaning out the window three stories up preparing a second brick.

He stopped when I yelled, "Henry, what do you think you're doing? You could have killed me."

"Hey, Old Jack, who's going to miss you?"

"I'll deal with you, young man."

I went directly to the VMI commandant, Col. Adams. I related the incident and Henry was dismissed from the institution. I sighted Henry later that day on campus.

"Hey, Tom Fool, it's not over yet. You might have been a war hero, but you haven't seen the likes of Harmful Henry. I think we should have an old time duel. You're a coward, and I'm challenging you."

"I'll deal with you, Henry."

I went to the magistrate for a warrant of peace against Henry. Henry always dodged the magistrate preventing the serving of the peace warrant. He spotted me on campus a day later.

"Hey, Old Tom Fool, when are you giving me satisfaction? If you don't give me satisfaction by tomorrow, I'll kill you on sight. Tomorrow at one o'clock I'll be looking for you."

I did not show up for the duel so Henry continued to spread the word that I was a coward. He continued to change the dueling time daily. Finally, David Thoreau, a classmate of Henry, approached me one day after class.

"Master Jackson, Henry remains on campus, and the magistrate has not served him with your warrant. He continues to set new times for the duel."

"David, it appears the magistrate is in no hurry to serve the warrant. I am at a disadvantage dealing with Henry. However, Henry's a scrappy lad, and he's beginning to annoy me. I've fought and killed many men in war, but this situation is different. It's a civil matter, and I'll tell you what I'm going to do. I'm going to carry my Mexican War service revolver on my person for defense, and I'll also start wearing my forage. You might inform Henry I'd kill him at the drop of a hat if he approaches me. If he doesn't have a hat, I'll lend him my forage."

"I'll tell him, Master Jackson."

Henry was a young immature lad, and I expected him to react to that statement. After David recounted my conversation to Henry, he left VMI. It was the last time Henry was a problem, and the incident gained me more respect from the cadets. Once Henry believed I was serious he disappeared, and other cadets concluded his bark was worse than his bite.

Elinor and I continued with our family planning, and at the end of the school year Elinor delivered a beautiful baby girl, Rebecca. She was the most special thing to have entered my life. It was a feeling better than a battlefield promotion. I came home at the end of each school day just to play with her in front of the fireplace. She was a daddy's girl, and it was even fun getting up at three o'clock in the morning for the nursing. As she grew I played with her more. One day, as we played, I noticed a red irritation forming on her face. It was the result of me rubbing my beard against her while we played. I shaved off my beard so it wouldn't happen again. The second member from our family planning was Thomas

Jonathan Jackson, Jr. being born eighteen months later, and he was a dandy. I experienced the feeling again as I did with Rebecca, and I had another playmate. Rebecca helped me play with Little Tom every evening after school. VMI had sheltered us from the rest of the world and enabled me to have descendants; however, the rest of the world closed in around us.

Our nation was a country divided over the issue of slavery. Franklin Pierce was elected president, and he had to deal with the issue. John Brown's activities as an abolitionist were well known concerning attempts to abolish slavery. He had been very active in Pennsylvania, Kansas and Canada. He was a problem for Pierce, and he had been an active campaigner for ten years now receiving national attention. We were aware that Pierce would have to resolve this problem.

This was the happiest period of my life, and Elinor and I enjoyed watching the two children grow. I had a good supply of lemons in VMI mess hall and exercised daily to maintain health and blood circulation. The children met me daily at the door for play activities, and I smothered them with kisses and belly raspberries.

I began to improve my teaching skills to make classes and learning fun experiences. The cadets did not like the memory methods for class recitations. Problem solving appeared to be the most appealing method for teaching and learning. They understood the manipulations of Natural Philosophy units to produce a sensible solution, and they understood graphical and mapping methods. I decided to employ the technique of what they understood combined with scientific concepts to increase their learning.

CHAPTER 4

▼

THE WAR

It was the year 1859. John Brown with a small band captured the federal arsenal at Harpers Ferry, Virginia. Once armed, Brown was hoping the Virginia slaves would join his rebellion; however, slaves were too terrified of their owners to join John Brown's band. Secretary of War, John Floyd, ordered Lieutenant General Robert E. Lee to take a military unit and resolve the matter, and Lee led a squad of Marines to Harpers Ferry. On arriving at the arsenal Lee found John Brown's band had taken hostages. Lee, realizing the gravity of the hostage situation, devised a plan to minimize the loss of lives. He ordered the marines to fix bayonets, and they approached the arsenal after dark. He led the marines through an unattended window in the back of the arsenal. Once inside the marines captured the arsenal with little resistance. John Brown was made an example to anyone attempting to seize a federal arsenal and hold hostages to achieve unlawful goals. Virginia hanged John Brown in December of that year, and many cadets under officer supervision attended his hanging.

John Brown's activities were looked upon as an attack on the slave owner. It represented the nation's morality and economic issues. The nation had reached maturity, and it wasn't moral to have slavery. The second issue was economics, which influence the redistribution of the labor force. Our government had granted the southern states the right to maintain slavery. The industrialized north had a labor shortage, and it needed cheap labor to develop infant industry. As slaves escaped their masters to make their ways to northern freedom, the factories employed them at low survival wages. The grateful slave worked hard in the factories away from the environmental elements of the fields. These economics was the major reasons for the war-between-the-states.

Lee would remain at Harpers Ferry, and I continued to teach at VMI. The slavery issue was building momentum, and the south was upset at the government's attempt to stop the spread of slavery. They feared the uprising of their slaves to gain freedom. Abraham Lincoln was against slavery and when he was elected president, the Southerners feared an uprising even more.

Military academies continued to graduate young officers, and the majority of the graduates were from the southern states. Farming was a hard and dwindling industry, and the young southern boys wanted a more chivalrous life as officers. On the other hand the northern industry needed its sons as industrialists. The growing industry offered a more profitable life compared to being an officer.

Gen. Lee came to VMI to deliver a series of lectures, and we renewed our acquaintance.

"Well, Tom. It appears that we may have a revolution in this country over slavery and economics. The south is bitter over the new tax laws protecting northern industry. These issues could tear this country apart."

"You're right. When it happens I think Virginia will go with the south."

"Virginia has long roots developing this country. But Virginians don't support these new taxes the government is imposing. They have nothing to gain from them."

"I think you're right."

"Tom, are you coming to the auditorium tomorrow to hear my lecture?"

"You know I wouldn't miss it for the world. A team of army mules couldn't keep me away."

Gen. Beauregard led a group of South Carolinians to attack Fort Sumter in April 1861. After subjecting the fort to two days of cannon batteries, it surrendered. I knew it was the beginning of war. South Carolina and Texas had already withdrew from the union, and I knew other states would soon follow. Each incident drew me nearer my destination and involvement in the war. Texas wanted independence, and it didn't surprise me that they were the first to join South Carolina in withdrawing from the union.

Late in April, President Lincoln declared the existence of an insurrection and recruited volunteers for military service. South Carolina and seven other southern states withdrew from the Union and Lincoln instituted a naval blockade of the entire southern coast. Later that month Virginia joined the seceding southern states, and Lee resigned his commission in the Federal army to accept command of Virginia's military forces.

Jefferson Davis was elected president of the Confederate States of America. He appointed himself as commander-in-chief and made Lee brigadier general. I knew it was my duty to join Lee and support the south, and I resigned my teaching position and enlisted in the Confederate army. The school year was drawing to a close, and my children were growing up. They were attending school, and I had enjoyed their company every evening by the fireplace all winter. It would be the last winter I would spend with them. The next two months passed fast, and we decided Elinor would take the children to Clarksburg and live with her family. The mountain atmosphere would be good for the children, and they would be exposed to fewer hostilities when war started. I rode to Richmond to join Lee and Jefferson Davis.

I arrived in Richmond two days later and immediately arranged a meeting with Lee and Davis. President Davis accepted my application into the southern military, and I was commissioned a Major General and joined Lee's army. My first assignment was the defense of Virginia's Shenandoah Valley. A. P. Hill arrived in Richmond two months later demanding to become a general in the Confederate Army, and Davis made him a colonel in the infantry. He had lost all the revolvers and knives he had worn in the Mexican War. He also lost the young Mexican maidens; however, it was good to see him. We reminisced about the war and our short time together. We were assigned to Gen. Joseph Johnston's command, and I was in charge of the artillery, and Hill had the light brigade. Again, he found his own circle of officers excluding me. He talked with me only at planning and staging times prior to battle.

I began my defense assignment of the Shenandoah Valley. I set about my first duty in finding an expert mapmaker. A mapmaker was essential to the artillery. The terrain and firing distances had to be known for planning attacks and positioning cannons. The mapmaker would efficiently help me command the two thousand troops at Winchester. Preservation of the valley was essential for if the valley was lost, Virginia was lost. If Virginia was lost the Confederacy was lost. Shenandoah Valley controlled by the Confederate Army would always be a threat to Washington, and I would ensure the valley remained in Confederate control. It was my mission.

General Joe Johnston divided his army into four brigades in Winchester. Bee, Bartow, Elzey and I commanded these brigades, and my assignment was to occupy Union generals Pope, Banks, Kelly and Rosecran to prevent them from uniting with McClellan. Banks' unit with seventeen thousand men, Rosecran with twenty-two thousand men and Kelly with five thousand surrounded my army. I had to create confusion among these forces to sustain the Confederate Army, and Kelly was the greatest threat to my existence. I had learned my lessons well at the Academy and in the Mexican War. The Academy taught classical offensive and defensive campaigns, and I new we weren't equipped to perform these maneuvers. However, I knew what they were taught, and the methods they would employ. We had VMI cannons against the latest riffled cannons developed by the industrial machinery of the United States Army. I knew the northern generals and how they were planning to fight this war, and I would use this knowledge against them. I would fight these battles with speed, cunning and deception. I knew my enemy for I had studied and fought with him.

My first orders were to engage the enemy in Bath, and I marched my regiment with artillery toward Bath some forty miles south of Winchester. The weather was accommodating, and the men began to shed their heavy winter garments during the march. However, the further we marched the colder it became, and by the time we reached Pughtown we were freezing. We had managed ten miles, and we woke up to a blizzard the next day and pushed onto Bath. We reached Unger's store and the soldiers were tired and hungry. The supply wagon had fallen behind after being caught up in the storm. The next day we entered the outskirts of Bath. The Union troops had fled leaving a small force present, and we dispatched a small contingency to demand the surrender of the town. The Federals refused our offer so I set up my artillery on the town's outskirts and began shelling the enemy positions. The Union soldiers were reinforced the next day, and I withdrew toward Romney. For the next few days the weather was bitter, and the men became hungry and cold. The march to Romney took two days, and we halted again at Unger's store to regroup and take care of the horses.

My headquarters were in Winchester, and I could not afford being cut off from Johnston's army. McClellan had station forces in Cumberland, Romney, and Hancock for the opportunity to take possession of Winchester for it was the key town to the Shenandoah Valley. I knew that Romney had fewer troops assigned there making it the opportune place to relieve a thorn in my side. We left Unger's store on the fourth day. It was sleeting, and by the time we arrived in Romney the men were covered with ice. Union troops fled Romney thinking our forces were larger than we actually were the day before we arrived, and I ordered my troops into winter quarters.

Gen. Loring's troops remained in Romney. A small brigade was placed in Bath to prevent Union troops crossing at Hancock, and I took my brigade back to Winchester and was later joined by Loring's brigade. He was more comfortable in

Winchester not fearing being cut off by Federal troops. I was settled in my officers quarters early one morning when my aid escorted a Confederate officer, Maj. John Mosby, into my quarters. He saluted.

"Good Morning, Gen. Jackson. I thought I would come by to see if you were still square rooting."

"Mosby, it's great to see you. Sit down and bring me to date on your involvement in the war and your life."

"Ah pshaw, Tom. Let me say I've missed you. I haven't seen you since the wedding and leaving the Academy. How is Mary anyway?"

"John, Mary's dead. She's been dead about thirteen years now. I married Elinor Junkin from my hometown, and we have two children. Mary died in New York City while I was in the Mexican War. How have you been? What have you been doing all these years since the Academy?"

"Well, before the war, I was a lawyer in Abingdon, VA. I never thought I'd be in the Confederate Calvary. In fact, I'm really in the service of Virginia for Virginia is the heart of these American states. This is where it really began with the British, and it was Virginia leading the way against the British. You're in my country, and I protect the Virginia people. This is Mosby country."

"That sounds good, John. We have a lot of catching up to do. I'll tell you about my encounters with Hiram and Hill in Mexico. Let's get some dinner."

At dinner soldiers gathered around Mosby's table just to be near him. Civilians and troops alike loved him. He would have great conflict with Gen. Custer over hanging captured Confederate troops, and he would later become a good friend of Grant over the incident. After dinner back in my quarters I resumed my encounters in the Mexican War. I began.

"John, the Mexican women were great. Hiram and Hill became very involved with those raven-haired beauties. Hill showed up two weeks late to relieve me when I was given leave at Mary's death. He showed up dressed like a Mexican bandito with a half dozen revolvers and four or five swords and knives. Hiram was our quartermaster, and he kept me supplied with lemons and munitions. I became a major in the regular army before leaving to come back to New York. I had to stay overnight in New Orleans, and I spent that night with Hiram."

"Tom, I haven't been in contact with anyone until now. You're the first one I've seen since the Academy."

"You'll be seeing Hill. He's assigned to Johnston's unit."

The next day I received orders to advance to Manassas near Bull Run. I arrived in Manassas two days later to find Gen. Lee preparing a major attack on Gen. Meade at Bull Run. We gathered in Lee's tent that evening for instructions. Bee,

Hill and Johnston were in attendance, and Hill was courteous. He had been spending much time recovering from his prostate problem. Lee began.

"Tom, I want you to position your artillery and men on Henry Hill. Have your men lie down on the opposite side of the hill, and when Union troops transverse the top of the hill your unit will open fire. Gen. Bee will defend the ridge next to Henry Hill. Col. Hill, you lead the calvary from the left flank. Any questions?"

All Lee's instructions were right out of the book at the Academy. Daylight began with heavy artillery fire from Union forces to the ridge occupied by Gen. Bee's brigade. Cannon smoke arose from their cannons, which were out of my artillery range. It's clear now that I should have kept those ships cannons. At noon his remaining men laid down in trenches after withstanding Federal artillery fire for five hours, and he came to Henry Hill to confer with me on combining our troops. He had suffered losses, and I agreed to the combination. He returned to his troops.

"Men, we're going to join forces with Gen. Jackson's Brigade. Look at them. They're standing a stonewall on Henry Hill. Let's join them and become part of that stonewall." There began the name Stonewall for me from that time on.

Federal troops advanced onto Henry Hill, and our troops rose from a lying position. We fired with our howitzers and rifles laying them low, and they retreated leaving us with our first real Confederate war victory. We had many battles, which resulted in a stalemate, but this was a real victory. My raids and quick hit maneuvers within enemy territories were successes, but they weren't considered victories. It was the beginning of the Stonewall Brigade and changing my name to Stonewall Jackson. We returned to Winchester after the Battle of Bull Run. Lincoln had increased Gen. Banks' army to thirty-eight thousand; however, Banks was not a formidable leader. He depended on mass force rather than leadership skills. He and McClellan had plans for him to push into the valley. Banks encountered little resistance in capturing Charles Town and Bunker Hill. I monitored Banks' actions for two weeks, and when he started his troops marching south toward Winchester, I moved my troops to guard the mountain passes and prevented Banks from cutting off Gen. Johnston. Winchester was a town occupied more than any other town during the War Between the States.

My army was small and mobile, and it could be in a fifty-mile radius in two days. It remained my job to protect Johnston to keep us operational in the Valley. Banks assigned Gen. Shield's nine thousand troops to defend Winchester while he joined McClellan. Their objective was to pursue Johnston, and I was beginning to see that my small army could not compete with masses at McClellan and

Banks disposal. My mobility wasn't enough to protect Gen. Johnston. We were at a showdown with Gen. Shields and Kernstown was the location. The resulting Battle of Kernstown was the only one I lost. We marched toward Kernstown to find Shields' army concentrated in the wheat field on the right of the turnpike supported by artillery on Prichard's Hill. I deployed troops to the right as a holding action, and the remaining troops I took to an unoccupied wooded area to eliminate escape to Winchester.

I pulled the artillery into place on the ridge, and the battle began. We beat the Union to gain advantage at a stone wall at the end of the ridge. We immediately defended the position on three assaults to discover that we were outgunned. I had underestimated the size of Shields forces for he had a major army, not just a rear guard. My aid returned to report Shields army consisted of ten thousand men. Shields deployed his men to direct his assault in the center of our forces. And we fought off the attacks again and again until the ammunition began to run out, forcing our withdrawal. Even in retreat Union troops knew we presented a clear and present danger. Lincoln ordered Gen. Banks to return to the valley and Gen. McDowell's forty thousand troops to remain in Manassas to protect Washington.

We retreated to Mount Jackson three days later, and I sent for Lee's mapmaker, Capt. Hotchkiss, to make an offensive and defensive map of the valley. Gen. Banks cautiously pursued, and at each river crossing I stationed Colonel Turner Ashby's cavalry to engage his forces. This gave the general the impression that the Stonewall Brigade was a sizeable force.

We combined our regiment with Gen. Ewell's in an attempt to prevent Banks from taking control of the supply railroads at Staunton. A tent city constructed at Rude Hill became our camp. Banks began moving toward Staunton, and I put my plan together to deal with his advances along the way. I moved my artillery at the pace one would expect to move calvary. Between Ashby's Calvary and my portable artillery, Banks had hell all the way to Staunton. By the time Banks arrived in Staunton I withdrew my men to Swift Run Gap, and while Banks tried to control Luray Valley, he lost track of me. Unable to locate my regiment Banks requested to combine his regiment with McClellan. At the same time my unit had developed an internal problem, and I now had to take time to deal with the problem. I had to replace Richard Garnett with Gen. Charles Winder, and we needed the discipline Winder would provide. Charles had Ashby's confidence and our unit needed an efficient calvary, and they were dynamic working together.

I received a letter from Gen. Lee instructing me to use Gen. Ewell's division to attack Banks to relieve the pressure he put on Frederickburg. Ewell crossed the

Blue Ridge Mountains and occupied Conrad's Store, and I ordered Ewell to prevent Banks from taking Staunton. Meanwhile, I moved my regiment to join Gen. Edward Johnson west of Staunton. Our combined forces were greater than the Union Gen. Milroy's forces, and we needed to attack Milroy before Gen. Fremont would reinforce him. Our attack on Milroy would prevent Fremont from joining forces with Banks.

I marched my army east to Mechums Station, and we boarded boxcars to Richmond. Two miles from Mechums Station we detrained and marched to Staunton. It was my plan to have everyone believe I was leaving the Valley. We arrived in Staunton and made camp around the town. Once Milroy knew I was with Gen. Johnson again he withdrew to the Alleghanies, and we pursued Milroy to McDowell. Gen. Johnson and I arrived outside McDowell at Sitlington Hill. Federal artillery was placed on a hill parallel to Sitlington Hill. The terrain of Sitlington Hill was too rough for us to get cannons in place. Gen. Johnson deployed his men on the hill, and I positioned my regiment to attack from across the Bull Pasture River. Gen. Shenck had assumed command of Milroy's forces, and he attacked the Confederate force on Sitlington Hill hoping to complete the battle before dark.

The first Federal attack broke Confederate ranks on the right, and I sent Taliaferro to reinforce Johnson. Union forces shifted to attack the center of the Confederate line, and the Twelfth Georgia brigade confronted them proving their worth. Despite heavy casualties they inflicted much destruction on the Blue Bellies. We held Sitlington Hill, and the Blue Bellies withdrew to McDowell under darkness. By morning they had retreated from McDowell. The Battle of McDowell victory prevented Banks and Fremont from joining forces at Staunton.

I returned to Winchester to be reunited with Major Mosby. We met in his quarters this time.

"Good afternoon, Major." I started.

"Good afternoon yourself. You old square rooter. How goes the war? You're building quite a reputation for yourself."

"It may be equal to yours. I hear you're really taking care of the citizens."

"Yes, I try. These people are having a hard time just living. The Federals take from them then we take what they have left. I've been accused of fighting under a black flag just looking after them. You know we have to leave them food to eat. The Blue Bellies left a family in Shepherdstown with a single milkcow to feed a baby."

"True. We're all having a hard time in this war."

"Tom, I plan to pester Gen. Pope by disrupting his supply line. I'm most effective at performing these activities; however, Custer is aggravating me. He killed a Confederate soldier while the soldier's mother begged for his life. He told the mother to get into her house before he killed her. I've penned a letter to his superior concerning his cowardice actions."

"Well. You remember George was always a squirrelly one at the Point."

I always enjoyed my visits with John. He was a warrior.

Back in my quarters my thoughts turned to Gen. Ewell. His regiment was still at Conrads Store keeping an eye on Banks, and I sent my aide to have him meet me at Mount Solon. The Mount Solon meeting would generate plans to attack Banks at Front Royal. Ewell's brigade met my regiment in New Market ten miles from Front Royal as planned. Ashby had gone to Buckton to disrupt Banks' communications from Front Royal, and we marched into Front Royal by Gooney Manor Road. When we reached the top of the hill at Front Royal, I could look down on the Union encampment on the South Fork of the Shenandoah River. For our campaign to be a success we needed to beat the Union Army to the river bridges to prevent their escape. A Union picket spotted our troop deployment, and he fired a warning shot allowing the Blue Bellies to retreat to a hill north of town. The Union commander Kelly spotted the Confederate calvary moving in the direction of the river bridges during the attack of the hill, and he dispatched troops to move toward the bridges. Confederate troops arrived at the bridges allowing the Union troops to escape. Union troops set fire to the bridges but not in time to destroy them before Confederate troops could cross.

On the other side of the river I saw the Union troops escaping toward Winchester. I ordered Lt. Col. Thomas Flournoy with his calvary to pursue Kelly's unit. After three miles Federal troops took a defensive stance in Cedarville. Flournoy continued pursuit and attack until the Federal troops surrendered, and we captured seven hundred fifty prisoners. Banks hunkered down, and this was where I wanted him to be. He was still in Strasberg awaiting an attack from the south, and once he learned Front Royal was under attack he thought it was a feint action. Even after I had taken Front Royal he remained put. In order to keep Banks occupied I sent the calvary to take a small hill nearby, and this action confirmed with Banks that the attack would come from the south. Finally, Banks decided to occupy Winchester, and I sent Ashby's calvary to observe Banks' movements from Strasburg. I also detached Ewell's regiment to Newtown to observe the enemy's movement up the Valley Pike. A courier from Ewell's calvary informed me that Union supply wagons were on the road to Winchester, and it was now time to strike Banks' military unit. It was a race to Winchester.

I left Gen. Ewell in Cedarville as reserves, and we begin our march to Winchester. It was a slow march, and we had to stop occasionally to fight the First Maine and First Vermont units. Finally, Banks' army was in view retreating to Winchester, and the road was filled with wagons and troops. It was time to teach Banks a lesson in artillery maneuvers. I stationed my artillery and opened fire on the road. The devastation I brought on Banks was unbelievable. It was like a massive hog slaughter only with people and horses. Banks' calvary installed cannons south of our location, and they opened fire to relieve the pressure I had put on his unit. I dispatched Ashby with artillery support to pursue the retreating Union troops and to show them no mercy. The Blue Bellies vanished indicating a feint, and I realized then that Banks had escaped. I dispatched my aide to Gen. Ewell to prepare for battle south of Winchester, and I ordered my infantry to race toward Winchester without rest. I knew I must join Ewell with artillery support when he engaged Banks.

Daybreak was the beginning of the first Battle of Winchester. Winder and the Stonewall brigade were to take the hill controlling the turnpike. While Ewell began the battle, Winder's unit took the hill. Winder's unit came under heavy fire from Banks' forces across from a second ridge. Union cannons delivered their deadly parcels. I ordered Taylor's unit to take the second ridge, and he took the ridge by a flank. The regiment courageously surged forward to be met by destructive volleys of grape from the Union troops. The unit charged the hill in a grand military manner, and Ewell flanked the left side of Banks' unit sending the Blue Bellies fleeing through the streets of Winchester.

I ordered the troops to pursue the fleeing Union Army until they reached the Potomac. The Federal troops never stopped until they reached the other side of the Potomac. We had won an important victory forcing Lincoln to make changes in his plans. He was worried about the safety of Washington, and I had put the fear into Lincoln. I wanted Gen. Lee to commission me to attack Lincoln's headquarters in Washington, but he never granted me the privilege. Lee's actions denoted he had no intentions of overthrowing the Federal government.

Sooner or later I knew Lincoln would have to deal with me. He repositioned Fremont to Strasburg, and Gen. McDowell was ordered to Front Royal to prevent me from escaping to the south. His plan was to destroy my army. Union Gen. Shields captured Front Royal, and Fremont began his attack from Middletown. I was following Lee's orders to demonstrate against Harpers Ferry. The Army of the Valley was ordered south, and I assigned the Stonewall Brigade to Harpers Ferry as I approached Winchester. It became necessary to recall the Stonewall Brigade to Winchester. The Brigade hunkered down in Winchester to access the actions of Fremont, Banks and McDowell. Their movements were so inefficient that I was unable to conclude anything from their actions. They weren't following any military tactic. It was almost as if there were thousands of men on a camp outing.

Bad news came from the Battle of Seven Pines when Gen. Johnston engaged McClellan. Johnston was mortally wounded, and Gen. Robert E. Lee became his replacement.

The Army of the Valley had begun its movement south, and Gen. Ewell engaged Fremont at Strasburg allowing the Stonewall Brigade to pass. Fremont applied much resistance until Gen. Taylor's men attacked his flank, and the union troops scattered like sheep. After occupying Strasburg the Stonewall Brigade continued their retreat south. After we crossed the North Fork Bridge we burned it and camped again at Rude's Hill. The next few days we pushed to Port Republic. Gen. Fremont constantly pursued our retreat with Gen. Ashby continuously defending our rear against him and Bayard's calvary. He was successful to the point of being taken out by a Pennsylvania sharpshooter. He was a tremendous loss to the Army of the Valley.

I found my army to be caught between two Union forces, Fremont's and Shields'. Fremont continued to pursue our rear, and Shields pursued from the Luray Valley direction. These forces were headed for a showdown at Port Republic. It was time for my mapmaker to earn his keep, and he found the terrain complex. Port Republic was located between the North and South Rivers, and the rivers joined northeast of Port Republic to form the south fork of the Shenandoah Rivers. There was a wooden bridge over the North River northwest of the Village. At the northeastern end of the village there were fords across the South River, and Shields would have to cross at one of these fords to reach Port Republic. I situated my army along the bluffs overlooking Port Republic and the North River. This location allows our artillery to command the village and the South River fords, and I assigned Gen. Ewell to protect our rear at Cross Keys when Fremont attacked.

It took Fremont two days to prepare his attack on Port Republic. At the first onslaught he marched his troops across South River into Port Republic overpowering my guards at the bridge. Immediately they set up artillery at the bridge, and I yelled at Colonel Carrol.

"Take out 'em damn cannons at the bridge!"

"'Em are our cannons, sir." He hesitated to review the cannon installations.

"No they're not! I just watched the Blue Bellies install them. Now begin firing! They just elevated 'em cannons in our direction."

The artillery duel began, and in the meantime I had located Colonel Fulkerson.

"Colonel! Charge the bridge with your Virginia regiment."

"Yes sir!" He was off at once with his brigade.

The bridge was cleared leaving that avenue for escape. As the Federal troops retreated Gen. Fremont began his assault on Ewell. Gen. Ewell's troops maintained position when the Federals opened their artillery attack. His army was deployed in the woods in front of a small creek which the Union troops had to cross. He deployed four batteries of artillery and two regiment brigades under the leadership of Gen. Elzy. As the artillery battle raged I could see the Union army beginning to advance and attack. I had placed Gen. Trimble in command of the troops in that area. He was a seasoned officer, and his troops held fire until Union troops were directly in their firing line. His firing command sent a hail of lead slowing their initial attack. As they regrouped he sent a second volley creating panic among the remaining troops, and the second volley made the survivors retreat at such a pace that the supporting troops also retreated. Fremont's army outnumbered ours two to one, and I expected a second attack on Ewell's position. It never came. Gen. Thimble, a crusty old man of sixty, spotted Union artillery and ordered his men to seize the unit. It was a half-mile away and before ground troops could engage, the cannon crew escaped. I summoned Ewell and Thimble to my tent.

"Gentlemen, we have routed the enemy once again."

"Gen. Jackson, allow me to night attack Fremont before he can plan further strategy."

"Gen. Thimble, our forces cannot support a night action. The Blue Bellies still outnumber us."

"Your courage is admired, Gen. Thimble. However, I must agree with Gen. Ewell."

The Battle of Cross Keys ended with Gen. Ewells troops standing between Fremont and Port Republic.

I remained trapped between two Union armies, and I devised a plan to defeat both. I brought the majority of Ewell's command to Port Republic and left Thimble and Patton to hassle Fremont. I would attack Gen. Shields first then defeat Fremont. I met with Winder and the Stonewall Brigade as soon as they crossed the North River into Port Republic.

"Gen. Winder, have your men cross the South River on the newly constructed bridge. After the troops cross the bridge march them toward Conrads store and search for Gen. Shields."

Gen. Winder performed as planned. He finally spotted Union troops in a wheat field behind a double row fence, and he immediately attacked to dispense Shields' army. Winder and the Stonewall Brigade begin the attack by charging the Union line across the wheat field. I had not anticipated the Union artillery, which opened fire from the right followed by a volley from Shields infantry inflicting causalities on the Stonewall Brigade. It was a trap similar to Kernstown, and we fell back to regroup. I spotted the Union artillery on a small hill to my right.

"Gen. Winder, take two regiments through the undergrowth and capture the artillery position."

"Yes Sir!"

His units advanced through the thick undergrowth to within one hundred yards of the Union artillery. Immediately, Winder spotted three regiments of Union infantry supporting the artillery. His first volley drove the artillery back, and Union infantry volleys allowed the artillerists to turn their cannons and fire on us. Outnumbered, the Stonewall Brigade failed to take the cannon position, and I had lost my chance to defeat Shields and Fremont in the same day. I sent the command to Thimble to retreat across the bridge and burn it. This would keep Fremont on the other side of the river while I battled with Shields. After burning the bridge, Thimble joined me in the fight against Shields. I knew we needed reinforcements immediately, and I had forgotten about Col. Hays and the Louisiana men of the Taylor's Brigade. They were making a river crossing at a previously constructed makeshift wagon bridge. Once across they made way to the battleground, and I engaged Col. Hays immediately.

"Colonel, reinforce Winder's Stonewall Brigade!"

"Yes Sir!"

"Thank you, Colonel. Your regiment is an answered prayer."

He ordered his troops into action. Gen. Taylor arrived with the remainder of his brigade and we developed a plan to silence the Union cannons.

"Gen. Taylor, take your infantry around to the right, and let your marksmen pick off the artillery men. Have them perform a simultaneous volley before they know you're in the vicinity."

We were not out of the woods yet, and Union troops were mounting a charge. Winder informed me that he could not withstand a charge, and I agreed that we perform a charge first. Winder and Hays' troops quickly begin the charge by racing across the field to a fence before Union fire forced them to the ground. The Blue Bellies continued to rain fire upon the pinned Stonewall Brigade, and with no protection the unit broke running to the rear. Gen. Ewell saved the day by arriving on the scene and attacking the enemy's left flank, and Union forces fell back and regrouped. They renewed the attack on Ewell's troops, driving them into the woods near the hill where Union cannons were deployed. Ewell immediately recognized an opportunity to seize the Union cannon and begin to advance up the hill. Meanwhile, Taylor's men were in position to deploy when they heard a Federal cheer indicating my position was under fire and pressed. He ordered a charge and the Confederates rushed forth yelling. His men charged forth twice in hand to hand combat, and each time they were beaten back. He regrouped his men and ordered a successful third charge. The fighting was brutal, and they had a short celebration. Just as the celebrating died down, Tyler brought his Ohio regiment up the mountainside, and Taylor's men set their backs to the mountainside and prepared for battle. The air was filled with the smell of sulfur and death.

Ewell engaged the infantry and artillery at the same time Tyler began his charge. It was a short battle, and Ewell had the Union cannons in his control. Tyler realized now that he was outgunned, and he retreated to join Shields' main force. The newly acquired artillery was now directed at Shields' army in the field below. Additional reinforcements arrived under the command of Taliaferro, and the Union troops began a slow retreat north. Afterwards Fremont and Shields retreated to Mount Jackson and Luray I moved to Brown's Gap and later to Weyer's Cave. This movement concluded the end of the Valley Campaign. Lee summoned me to Richmond for further involvement. I had performed my task in the Valley by keeping the enemy occupied and not allowing Banks to join McClellan. Upon arriving in Richmond I learned John Mosby had been wounded and was recovering there. I proceeded directly to his quarters. He was awake when I made my entry.

"John, how are you?"

"Ah pshaw. Look who's here. It's the old square rooter. I'm recovering, Tom."

"What happened?"

"You're not going to believe this story. I was a dinner guest of a farmer outside of Winchester when Union calvary attacked the farmhouse. They were firing through every window, and I was shot in the shoulder. Realizing I was wounded I crawled into a nearby bedroom and removed my officer insignia identification just in time to be discovered by one of 'em Blue Bellies. He thought I was a wounded private and left me to die. After they rode away I was placed in a buggy and brought to Richmond, and I've been here for a week now. I should be back in action in another few months."

"John, everyone is accusing you of fighting under a black flag again. Is that true?"

"Tom, what are you trying to say? Do you think I'm a pirate? I continue to fight for the people of Virginia. When I run into Federal sympathizers I take from them what I need to continue fighting."

"Don't blame you. Haven't heard a bad word about you from any southerner. In fact, they renamed this area Mosby country, and they've even given you a nickname. They call you the Gray Ghost. They call you that because you disappear from the Union army just when you're cornered."

"That's the best news I've heard lately."

"I have to report to Gen. Lee for my new command. I wanted to see you first."

"Just one thing before you go. How many times have you square rooted since you've been in this war?"

We laughed, and I left to report to Lee. I arrived at Lee's headquarters. His orderly invited me to have a seat in his office, and he said Lee would arrive shortly. I made myself comfortable, and Gen. Lee made his entrance.

"How are you, Tom?"

"Very well, General. I completed my task at Port Republic and Cross Keyes."

"You did General. And you did a fine job. I would summarize your actions as a success in the Valley. You accomplished your overall objective, and you kept Gen. Banks from joining forces with McClellan. McClellan continues to perform as we anticipated. Lincoln keeps sending him more troops, and he keeps adding them to his bodyguard. I hope Lincoln doesn't get tired of his indecisiveness. Tom, tomorrow you, Hill, Longstreet and I will make plans to attack McClellan in Mechanicsville. I have a little surprise for him. Report back here at nine o'clock tomorrow for details. Have my orderly assign you proper quarters and get a good night's sleep."

"Thank you, sir. I'll see you tomorrow."

The orderly assigned me a sleeping room in the officers quarters, and I enjoyed a good ham dinner in the officer's mess. The orderly escorted me to Gen. Lee's headquarters promptly at nine o'clock. Hill and Longstreet had arrived, and Lee acknowledged my presence.

"Come in Gen. Jackson. You know Gen. Hill and Gen. Longstreet."

"Sure." I shook hands with the two generals. I received a warm welcome from Longstreet.

"Hill, it's good to see you again. I haven't seen you since the you replaced me in Mexico."

Lee interrupted, "Your reminiscing must wait until after our planning session. We have work to do."

Lee began to outline the attack plan.

"McClellan has forty thousand troops stationed along the Chickahominy River protecting the eleven bridges crossing the river. My army shall assail McClellan troops from the left. Tom, you must bring the Army of the Valley to Ashland and unite with part of Hill's brigade at Half Sink. You will march southward, and the remainder of Hill's brigade will cross Meadows Bridge and march toward Mechanicsville. Longstreet will fall in behind you crossing Meadows Bridge. Your combined forces will proceed down the north side of the Chickahominy attacking McClellan forces. I will attack McClellan's right and destroy his supply route at York River Railroad. This will cut McClellan off from his base and force him to fight at a disadvantage. Our plan is to attack on June 26. Tom, this means your army must be at Ashland on the twenty-sixth of June. Can you be there on time?"

"Yes sir, I'll be there."

"You've always been very dependable, and I believe if anyone can get the Army of the Valley there on time it's you."

"Thank you, sir." I noticed Hill's smirky smile.

"Does anyone have any questions?"

"That's a tight schedule." Longstreet stated. "Everything depends on Jackson being on time."

"I'm very aware of that. I'll make plans now to maneuver the Army of the Valley into position."

We concluded our visit at the officer's mess. I left on a two-day ride to meet the Army of the Valley the next morning. The following day I started the Army of the Valley marching toward Mechanicsville and the Chickahominy. We arrived in Ashland to join Hill at Half Sink. We arrive to find that Hill's Light Brigade had already crossed Meadows Bridge. He captured the Union sentries and forced the Federal army back to Mechanicsville. I continued the attack plan by proceeding to Hundley Corners at McClellan's rear. Hill pressed the attack forcing the Union army to Beaver Creek Dam. Here the Blue Bellies regrouped and entrenched with optimum gun placements. The Light Brigade attacked repeatedly suffering great losses before retreating to Mechanicsville.

Gen. Lee summoned his officers to meet him at Willis Church. He informed us that we would attack again at Malvern Hill, and we began the attack early the next day. The Battle of Malvern Hill was a stalemate. However, it ended McClellan's attempt to attack Richmond, and Hill's Light Brigade was left to guard Malvern Hill to eliminate any threat to Richmond. Lee invited us again to a meeting at Willis Church. He started with his communications from President Davis.

"Gentlemen, I want to bring you up to date on the war effort in the west. Davis tells me Lincoln has named thirty-four new generals, and guess who one of those generals is?"

No one answered.

"Well, I'm going to tell you. It's Grant. You remember Hiram Grant from the Academy? He must have quit drinking long enough for Lincoln to make him a general, and that's not all. He's having success in West Tennessee. He curtailed Harris's activity in disrupting Union supply lines, and his assignment is to keep Missouri, Kentucky and Tennessee pro-Union."

"General Lee, I know Grant. I served with him in the Mexican War. His real name is Hiram."

"Tom, call him whatever you like. He's successful."

"It must be his planning strategy, communications and terrain mapping."

"Gentlemen, Kentucky remains in the Union, and Lincoln thinks about the possibilities of Confederates invading it. Pres. Davis has assigned Gen. Polk to command Confederate activities in Tennessee, and Polk has already invaded and occupied Columbus, Kentucky. He can overlook and control the Mississippi River from his camp. Grant and Fremont had intentions of displacing Polk. Gen. Polk dispatched Gen. Pillow to engage the Union troops. Pillow engaged a small force commanded by Gen. Grant. He cut off Hiram's escape route and made him fight his way back to his boats on the Mississippi River to escape back to Paducah. Apparently Hiram didn't have time to plan this battle."

After the meeting was dismissed, Gen. Lee gave me directions for engagements with Gen. Pope in central Virginia.

"Jackson, I want you to take the Stonewall Brigade to Gordonville to maintain control of the railroad junction."

"Yes sir." I replied. I saluted and returned to my quarters.

The next day the Stonewall Brigade started the march to Gordonville. By the time I arrived, Lincoln had added another fifty thousand troops to Pope's army. Lee immediately responded by sending me the Light Brigade under the command of A. P. Hill. Three days later Hill showed up with the Light Brigade, his wife and family. His wife had started joining him almost always at each post for Hill always had a reputation for being a lady's man with the camp women at each battle site. His wife curtailed those activities, and the children loved having him at home. Union Gen. Banks moved a small force into north central Virginia near Orange. Pres. Davis was afraid the Federals were trying to reestablish control over the area, and he ordered me to remove Banks before they established control. Immediately, I organized the troops for the march from Gordonville to Orange. It was a dusty and hot march, and we made about eight miles a day. Hill constantly complained about the dust, ninety-degree temperature, and the file order the Light Brigade had to march. Finally, I sent his troops on an alternate route to Orange.

The third day as we were approaching Orange, Banks' artillery sounded their welcome. We were within six miles of Orange, and my army had gained the advantage position of Slaughter Mountain. Federal troops remained in the plains below the mountain, and we wheeled our artillery into position. Our infantry moved forward from the front and on each side of the enemy. Federal troops concentrated and attacked to our left wave after wave. Each side was taking heavy losses, and Hill had not arrived on time from the alternate route. I sent Capt. Briggs to locate Hill, and Briggs had the Light Brigade to reinforce our left side. The added artillery dueled with Union ranks, and the Light Brigade occupied positions behind rail fences and rock walls. As Federal troops advanced, the added gun power checked their efficiency strewing the ground with bodies. The Light and Stonewall brigades begin to press the attack, and we marched forward relieving troops holding their positions during the bedlam. We pursued the retreating enemy to a wheat field. Here, Union reinforced troops were making a stand.

These new forces were holding until the Stonewall Brigade seized the opportunity to attack their flank. Banks made a final attempt to subdue the Confederates with a dual calvary charge from two directions. Again, the wheat field was strewn with Federal dead. Banks' army was in full retreat, and we gave chase until dark. Darkness always signaled the end to the day's confrontation. We returned to the wheat field to make camp for the night. With Banks retreating from northern Virginia we returned to Gordonville to join forces with Lee, and his army was positioned to keep Pope in check. Pope was positioned on the north bank of the Rapidan. Lee ordered Longstreet to attack his front, and the Stonewall Brigade to curl around for a flank attack. We marched through down pouring rain to the Rappahannock. The river was over the dam where we had intended to cross, and our engineers put in place a temporary bridge. It was time to attack Pope's rear, but first we burned the railroad-bridge, which delivered Pope's supplies at Bristoe Station. Then, we seized the stockpile of supplies, and everyone made efficient use of them. The men had two pairs of shoes each and plenty to eat. We rested at Pope's rear awaiting Lee's orders.

I moved my army to Groveton and sent Hill to Bull Run. Our first activity was an ambush of Gen. Rufus King's troops. We caught his infantry in artillery crossfire, and we detected Pope's troops to be on the move. At first we thought he was retreating, but the moves were too militarily organized. The capture of a courier revealed his plan to attack my unit. We spent the night digging earthworks and preparing for battle. Early the next day, Pope began the attack. His intent was to destroy my army before Lee could assist by attacking his front. However, Confederate fire was so strong and concentrated that the center of the Union line decayed. They suffered heavy losses and withdrew to the woods to regroup. They attacked again walking and falling over dead bodies as they advanced. Pope brought in four more divisions of seasoned veterans from previous battles under Gen. Hooker. They advanced, and my infantry laying in wait delivered volley after volley of deadly minie balls.

The battle raged on hand to hand, and infantry and artillery delivered devastating blows to the enemy. We repulsed several assaults, and the Union troops had become weary. Finally, Pope made one last assault before nightfall. He gathered his troops with reinforcements and made the charge, and we were almost out of ammunition. We fought gallantly with bayonets and muskets used as clubs, and when all seemed to be lost Gen. Jubal Early charged to our assistance with two brigades, driving the Blue Bellies into the woods and laying great waste to their army. I recalled Gen. Early to shore-up our defenses. The day ended with the sun slowly sinking, and we made piles of the dead bodies from the day's work.

The next day Pope renewed the attack, and we had reinforced our weakened lines. Federal troops marched in columns wave after wave and attacked my division. Our artillery opened up with round after round tearing apart their infantry. They advanced and we slaughtered them like hogs, and our batteries raked them at close range and the flag bearers kept advancing. Pope ordered another attack, and at that time Longstreet attacked his left flank and sent them reeling. Sensing victory, I rallied the troops to pursue the enemy while they were in full retreat. We celebrated the victory of a bloody battle. The weather changed and there was a downpour stripping the air clean of the gunpowder gases, and the men slept wherever they found a dry spot. It had been two weary days. I sent a messenger to Lee for further instructions, and the messenger returned with orders to continue pursuing Pope's army.

I moved the Stonewall Brigade north crossing Bull Run. My objective was to flank Pope at Fairfax Court House; however, the Stonewall Brigade was tired and bloody after the second Battle of Bull Run. They marched rapidly to the objective, and I tolerated the stragglers. We had to eliminate Pope before he could unite with McClellan. Hill with the Light Brigade was leading the charge, and his unit marched double-time. I ordered Hill to bivouac at Pleasant Valley Church to allow my division to accumulate. The men spent the night in an open field without dinner. It was Monday morning and the heavy rain continued. We marched four miles when the Light Brigade engaged Union troops at Ox Hill where Hill distributed the troops to increase his offensive efficiency. I turned the Stonewall Brigade south and ordered Ewell to do likewise to assist the Light Brigade. As we arrived at the battle scene another downpour occurred, and we were able to get off a couple rounds of musketry before our powder became soaked. The men fixed bayonets and fought the enemy with rocks and anything they put their hands on.

The rain poured and the thunder, lightning and cannon fire created a horrendous long remembered scene. A single Federal soldier rode into our lines and we demanded him to surrender. As he continued his ride a single musket volley to the head sent him reeling to the ground. It was the Union General Kearny. At Kearny's death the Battle of Chantilly was subdued, and Pope retreated. Lee summoned us to his headquarters.

"Men, we must give the troops a much deserved rest. We must attend our wounded before we can chase the Union army."

I asked, "What's the latest news from Davis?"

"Davis has been out of commission for three days with gout. Between him and Lincoln with their absenteeism, it's difficult to fight this war. It's good they're both absent at the same time. However, the last news I had from the western front was that Grant had taken Fort Henry on the Tennessee River. Luckily, the troops escaped to Fort Donelson. A few days later Grant, with the aid of Foote, attacked Fort Donelson on the Cumberland River forcing Gen. Buckner to surrender. These battles are the first major victories for the Union forces, and McClellan even sent congratulations to Grant. You remember how he used to feel about Grant at the Academy."

"What were our losses?" I asked.

"We surrendered fifteen thousand troops and five thousand horses along with many much needed supplies. Grant accepted unconditional surrender of the fort, and he's being hailed as Unconditional Surrender Grant. Needless to say Davis and I are very depressed by these Union victories. Lincoln has promoted Grant to major general."

I intervened, "Gen. Lee, the fall of Fort Donelson has exposed Nashville to the Union. Nashville is our major supply and industrial base."

"I know, Tom. This is why I'm greatly depressed. Two weeks after taking Fort Donelson Grant marched to Savannah, Tennessee uniting with Gen. Sherman at the Battle of Shiloh. Generals Johnston, Beauregard and Braggs initially routed Federal forces at Shiloh forcing them to retreat to Pittsburg Landing, and we continued to attack the Federal army the next day. However, Grant was able to rally his troops to counterattack, and Gen. Johnston was mortally wounded and Beauregard was placed in command. Gen. Beauregard retreated to Corinth, Mississippi. We were hoping for a victory here to retain control of Tennessee. This opens an opportunity for Federal troops to invade the heart of the South."

"You remember how Hiram always answered military battle questions at the Academy? He viewed war as if it were a chess game. He only had one fault and that was his drinking problem. He definitely liked his whiskey." I added my comments.

I returned to the Stonewall Brigade camp to find a soldier wanting to write home. It reminded me that I hadn't written Elinor in months, and I thought about the children.

"Excuse me, sir." The private saluted.

"What can I do for you, private?" I returned his salute.

"Could you help me write a letter to my family? I can't read or write."

"Sure. What's your name, private?"

"Noonam, sir. Private Thomas Noonam."

"Pleased to make your acquaintance, Tom."

Tom handed me the letter and I begin writing.

Dear Family,

We just completed two major battles. The first one was the second Battle of Bull Run. It was a bloody battle, but we prevailed again. We lost fifteen hundred men but they lost more. We chased the Union army to Fairfax Court House before we caught them. We fought them again running Gen. Pope out of the region.

It poured the rain during the second battle. We were so busy fighting that we hardly had time to eat. It's a good thing too because we don't have much to eat. I'd kill some game, but the powder is wet so that we're using bayonets on the enemy. We're so busy trying to keep dry that we hardly have time to think about anything else. It'd be nice to have a good night's sleep.

Here's my love to all the family.

Best regards,

Tom Noonam

"Tom, I wrote that you're doing well, and I gave some recent details of our battles. The next time we write I'll tell them hello for me."

"Thanks, general."

Again Gen. Lee summoned his commanders for another briefing.

"Gentlemen, we're going to invade the north. If we're successful we'll force Lincoln to negotiate a peace. It's possible to gain support from England or France if we take the initiative. Tomorrow, we'll march to the Potomac River at Leesburg. Dismissed."

I returned to the Stonewall Brigade and made ready for the march. The next day at four o'clock I rode inspection to ensure the troops were ready to march. The Light Brigade was not ready, and they casually filled their canteens in preparation for the march. At that moment Hill rode into camp, and I ordered him to make ready and begin the march. The Light Brigade begin marching at double-time, and the unit accrued many stragglers. I called for the noon procedure rest, and Hill continued marching. I ordered General Thomas to rest his men, and Hill continued to march with half the Light Brigade until he noticed the break in his ranks. He immediately turned his horse and rode in our direction. Upon his arrival he approached Gen. Thomas and demanded an explanation.

"Gen. Thomas, what's the meaning of this? Why are the men resting and not marching."

"You'd better ask Gen. Jackson standing under the tree with his horse."

Hill turned and started in my direction, and it was obvious he was upset.

"Why did you stop my men from marching?" He inquired.

"It was the noon procedure rest, and the men should be rested."

"You by-passed my command and went directly to a lower ranking officer, and this is not according to procedure. If you're going to give my men orders you don't need my services."

"Gen. Hill, consider yourself under field arrest. You will march at the rear of the Light Brigade on foot until we reach our destination."

"Might as well be at the rear of the Light Brigade. I never know your battle plans. They're always a secret."

"Hill, my battle plans are usually very simple. They're all based on the Academy's teachings. First, you find the objective and prepare for battle by classical methods. I wasn't aware you required so many details. Had you spent more time studying at the Academy instead of gallivanting around New York City you'd have known my plans. Now, retire to the rear of the brigade."

We finally opened the wound, and it would never be closed again. I ordered General Branch to take over the Light Brigade, and we marched through Maryland with Hill at the rear of his division. My army issued horse was a mare, which I affectionately named Little Sorrell after my mount at the Academy. She was being reshod one morning, and I had to use an unfamiliar stallion. I climbed into the saddle, and the horse began to buck. Finally, it reared up and fell backwards on me. I was helped from the ground and carried to my tent. Just as I was recovering from being bucked off the horse Major Paxton arrived with a note from Hill. The note read:

> I respectfully request you document the charges against me so that I may defend myself in a court martial. In the meantime I request to be returned to command the Light Brigade.
>
> Respectfully,
>
> Gen. A.P. Hill

I responded with a note back to Gen. Hill. The note read:

> The situation at hand is not worthy of a service court martial. In the event it becomes so, you will be charged in accordance to army regulations. You must remain with your division.
>
> Sincerely,
>
> Gen. Thomas J. Jackson

Just as I finished the Hill ordeal, Gen. Pender came into my tent. He saluted and began.

"Gen. Jackson, the men need rest and better food. They are worn, dirty and ragged, and they've been living off corn roasted in the shucking."

"General, we have to make do with the best we have. It saddens me for the troops. We are anticipating an attack from the north. Marylanders are not exactly Confederate sympathizers, and we're trying to win them over and our advances are slower than expected. McClellan is back in charge of the ninety thousand-man Army of the Potomac advancing on Fredericksburg. There remains a sizable Union force occupying Harpers Ferry blocking our line of communication and retreat."

I already had orders from Lee, and I was to march upon Harpers Ferry. My objective was to secure the arsenal to keep the gateway open to Shenandoah Valley. We were to begin the march upon Harpers Ferry in two days. The two days in preparation passed fast, and there was constant complaining over the lack of food. We started the sixty-mile march to Harpers Ferry. I rode back to check on Hill to find him riding in the ambulance. He was recovering from an attack of prostatitis, the result of the disease he contacted at the Academy. I knew I would need him in the upcoming battles; however, I had to keep control of his division to obtain the objective. A day later a messenger approached me with a message from Hill, and Hill asked to be returned to command his division in the upcoming battle. He requested to submit to arrest after the battle was over. I knew we had to deal with McClellan, and I much needed Hill to lead the Light Brigade. I restored Hill and sent word to Gen. Branch that Hill would be in command of the Light Brigade.

The next morning we crossed the Potomac at Lights Ford, and I positioned my forces to prevent the Federals stationed at Martinsburg from escaping westward. The Light Brigade marched towards Martinsburg to find the Blue Bellies under Gen. White had escaped during the night. The Light Brigade found goods and supplies in abundances left within the town, and the soldiers who had been living off of parched corn ate their fill. They loaded horses with supplies and continued their march to Harpers Ferry. Upon arriving in the vicinity the Stonewall Brigade positioned artillery on Loudoun Heights and Maryland Heights on the Potomac. This would render Harpers Ferry almost defenseless, and the Light Brigade was positioned west of the Federals. The Light Brigade withstood light action by Union infantry while the cannons were put in place.

In the afternoon I gave the command for the Light Brigade to attack the Blue Bellies on the left with support from artillery from Bolivar Heights. Hill opened up on Union troops trapped in an open meadow, and I begin artillery shelling from the two height positions. Federal troops could be seen scurrying retreat through the meadow. Gen. Pender moved to the left again to dispatch unsupported Union infantry, and the Light Brigade turned its artillery onto Gen. White's infantry and the ensuing bombardment proved to triumph. We were awakened with a heavy fog the next morning. We started shelling the Union positions and they returned fire. As the fog lifted we increased artillery fire on the Union positions. Our artillery fire was successful, and Gen. Pender started the infantry advance. Suddenly, a Federal soldier advanced from the ranks with flag of truce, and the shelling ceased to review the white flag.

Lt. Chamberlayne was dispatched into the Blue Belly line for the review. He made contact with Union Gen. White who requested to be escorted to Confederate lines for terms of surrender. He was taken to the schoolhouse on Charles Town pike where I had made temporary headquarters. Gen. White requested terms of surrender, and my response was "unconditional" surrender. My demand was as good as Hiram's, and I could grant indulgence later on.

"These are my terms, Gen. White. Your men will keep overcoats, blankets and sidearms. We shall provide rations, and your men must not serve in the Union army until exchanged."

The surrender was acceptable to both sides, and I assigned Gen. Pender to parole the prisoners. Hill was sent into Harpers Ferry to investigate the remains, and it lay in ruins. We captured artillery, rifles, powder, stores and much bounty. Hungry Confederate soldiers gorged themselves on the delicacies left by the Union army. They even outfitted themselves in new Blue Belly uniforms. I turned my attention to joining Lee's army to the north for we eventually had to deal with McClellan's army. That night the men rested, and an unfortunate incident occurred. Unbeknown to both Lee and me the status of our forces were delivered to McClellan in the form of three cigars wrapped in a hand written note prepared by Gen. Lee. The note contained the magnitude and fragmentation of our army. The note had been taken from a captured courier, and McClellan was probably surprised to find so few southern troops were causing so much resistance. The note also related Lee's planned activities in Maryland. This was one of Lee's great failures during the war. I never wrote or conveyed battle plans to anyone not even my officers. However, Lee made more than one mistake during this war. And his soldiers and southerners always forgave him. It was always my opinion that he never really wanted to win the war. He was more interested in using politics to make gains for the south.

These plans described our locations and number of troops. The Army of Northern Virginia was segmented into five units located approximately ten miles apart; however, fortunately for us McClellan hesitated again. Finally he moved on Longstreet and Harvey Hill in South Mountain securing the mountain pass at Boonsboro. We marched to Sharpsburg to combine our forces with Lee's army. McClellan moved the Army of the Potomac toward Antietam Creek, and Lee reacted by deploying the Confederate Army from the Potomac River to Antietam Creek. Lee's strategy prevented McClellan from bringing his artillery across the Potomac River, and the river was too deep for floating cannons across.

Gen. Lee deployed our combined forces of twenty-five thousand men, and he sent a courier to Harpers Ferry for Hill to bring reinforcements. Again, McClellan was slow to act, and he was using the time to position his army of a hundred thousand men to optimum performance. The time allowed Hill to march six hours to Shepherdstown. The Light Brigade arrived dressed in new uniforms acquired at Harpers Ferry and supplies from Union quartermaster stores. They were a welcome sight for the town's people and us. McClellan's artillery began pounding our left and center when Hill arrived. Gen. Burnside's Corp attacked a Georgia unit on the right, and he was pushing it back when Hill came over the hill with another six thousand men. Hill's Light Brigade on the right reinforced our men, and I turned six of my artillery pieces to the right to allow the Light Brigade to enter the battle and position their cannons. We had withstood great losses until the Light Brigade arrived. Our troops had fought valiantly against the overwhelming Federals, and the Blue Bellies continued to advance wave after wave. The artillerist blasted away canister after canister and each fuselage left a gaping hole in the Federal lines. Their advances were too fast to reload the hot cannons, and our artillerist retreated to the rear of the lines leaving the cannons to the Federals.

Our armies came together hand to hand in the cornfield, and our cannons continued to deliver canisters at each opportunity. Five hundred Union troops were immediately taken out in cannon crossfire, and muskets were loaded and fired so often that they became too hot to hold. Musket fire was so dense that it cut down the standing corn stalks. Hill's reinforcements drove Burnside's unit back across Antietam Creek, and McClellan pulled back his forces. The sun had begun to set, and later that night we heard the wounded laying in the field moaning and dying. It was a sound we had experienced before, and it was the agony of war. The Battle of Antietam Creek was a stalemate, and it was the bloodiest battle of the war. However, it allowed us to keep fighting for the next two and a half years. For this reason it was considered a Confederate victory, and we needed victories to supplement our exhausting finances. We were unable to promote European support for the south. It rained the next day, and an armistice gave us time to recover the wounded and bury the dead. We marched to Virginia for supplies and artillery while a Pennsylvania unit followed attacking our rear. The inexperienced unit was dispatched within two hours. They were caught up in musket and cannon fire, and their bodies floated down the Potomac River to Harpers Ferry. A break in the fighting allowed my argument to renew with Gen. Hill.

We marched toward Fredricksburg, and Gen. Lee made camp at Bunker Hill Inn, ten miles from the Antietam battleground. He gathered his command into the inn that evening for dinner. It had been weeks since we had a good home cooked meal. After small talk around dinner we gathered around the parlor fireplace for more formal conversation.

"Gentlemen, we've received another communications from Pres. Davis concerning the war in the west. I try to pass these along to you verbatim as I receive them." He began. "You know we must get assistance from Europe to make this a prolonged war for our resources are limited. The new conscripts enabled us to fight a good battle at Antietam. It was good soldiering and tactics, which made us prevail against overwhelming odds. We were outgunned in the artillery arena; however, cannon maneuvers by Jackson and Hill's units equaled anything the Federals threw at us."

I interrupted, "We didn't get a chance to capture any of their guns either."

"You're right, Tom. We usually capture eight or ten cannons at each battle." Lee replied. "You know I must get on with this unpleasant task of reporting the news from the west. It seems that one of Lincoln's new generals is fast making a name for himself. It's Ulysses Grant again, and he has taken Vicksburg. Initially, it was thought that it would be impossible to conquer Vicksburg; however, Grant is a resourceful general. Vicksburg is strategically located on the Mississippi River controlling Union movement and supplies along the river. Grant's first attempt to take the city was unsuccessful, and the miserable rainy weather worked to our benefit there. Also, it was reported diseases spread through his men leaving him with reduced forces for his attacks. Lincoln reinforced Grant's division with additional conscripted troops for a second attempt at taking Vicksburg, and Gen. Sherman was sent to join Grant. Both generals were surprised at Vicksburg's fortifications, and the second attack started similar to Grant's first battle. Again the Blue Bellies could make no progress, and Grant dug in around the city to control the supplies shipments. There was a fifty day standoff before Vicksburg was completely without food. Confederates were eating mule meat before they would surrender. Finally, Gen. Pemberton had to surrender Vicksburg. Grant paroled thirty thousand Confederate troops without their weapons at the surrender."

"Pemberton should have known to send out his calvary to hassle Grant's flank. Hiram cannot deal with a dynamic opposition."

"Stonewall, you're right. I wish I'd had a Stonewall at Vicksburg."

We were camped two days at Bunker Hill Inn when I received the first communication from Hill to deal with the injustice of his field arrest before the Battle of Antietam. The communication was directed through channels to Gen. Lee, and I penned my letter to Gen. Lee explaining Hill's failure to march several times when ordered. It was a matter of minor importance considering what we had just been through and the upcoming tasks lying in front of us, and I'd just as soon forget the whole matter. Lee had similar views toward Hill's request. He replied to Gen. Hill that the matter did not suffice an inquiry or court martial, and he anticipated the incidences would never be repeated again. Lee's reply infuriated Hill even more causing him to pursue the matter further. Hill's new request precipitated a meeting at the Boyd House, my headquarters. Here, Lee concluded the matter was settled, and it was not to be discussed henceforth. Hill and I coldly shook hands, and our future meetings were strictly military.

A few days later Lee divided the Army of Virginia into two corps, and Longstreet and I were promoted to lieutenant generals. We remained at Bunker Hill to treat our wounds, recruit enlistees and replenish our supplies. The soldiers bathed in the nearby Opequon River. I assigned Hill's unit to disrupt the Federals remaining in Shepherdstown by removing fifteen miles of C&O Railroad rails. It would be awhile before they could make repairs to receive supplies. Gen. Lee summoned me to his tent.

"Tom, Lincoln had replaced McClellan with Gen. Burnside, who has marched his troops to the heights of the Rappahannock overlooking Fredricksburg. I want you to proceed to Fredrickburg to confront him."

"Yes Sir. I'll prepare my men for the march."

It was a ten-day march through sleet and bad weather, and we finally arrived in Fredricksburg finding Burnside on the other side of the river waiting for pontoon boats to cross the river. I took the Stonewall Brigade to Lee's left and ordered Hill's unit to occupy the middle linking to Longstreet's Corp. The weather took a turn for the worse, and it snowed five inches and the troops had very few tents, blankets, and no boots. They suffered miserably. Many of the troops tied blankets around their feet to avoid frostbite. On Friday, Burnside opened fire with his artillery and began crossing the river on his pontoon boats.

Gen. Hill moved himself to the rear of his command and took to an ambulance. He was having another attack of prostatitis, the resultant disease that gave
him an excuse for not leading his troops. Hill's artillery and infantry were poorly
scattered leaving a huge area of underbrush, trees and swamp undefended. The
next morning Union Gen. Meade began the attack advancing on Hill's Light Brigade with five thousand troops. Gen. Pedham turned three cannon on the
advancing Union infantry pelting them with grape. Union artillery returned fire
removing a Confederate cannon, and Pedham continued to fire reeking destruction on the advancing Union army. The sulfur smell increased in the air from
each cannon fuselage. Again, Federal cannons returned fire until no more fire was
heard from Confederate guns. Meade believed rebel guns had been silenced and
ordered his infantry to attack the Light Brigade. Union infantry advanced within
one hundred yards of the Light Brigade when Pedham commanded his artillery
to open fire. All cannons under his command fired simultaneously raking Union
advancement. Pedham's artillery reloaded and fired a second fuselage at the
advancing foe.

Union infantry fell back and regrouped, and they advanced repeatedly suffering great losses. Everyone loaded and fired at will until the massive Union infantry pouring through unprotected gaps surrounded the cannons. The Federal
army had found the only weakness in what would have been the best defensive
position the Confederate army had encountered during the war. The massive
Federal army poured through the gap with muskets firing and fighting hand to
hand, and Confederate troops returned fire, running out of ammunition. Once
out of ammunitions they continued the battle with gun buts, bayonets and rocks.
Union troops continued to attack and advance until reinforced Confederate
troops fired a musket volley halting the attack. The battle raged with Meade's
massive infantry continuing to attack the Light Brigade. The Light Brigade was
yielding until Gen. Jubal Early arrived with his unit, and these Confederate soldiers arrived with the rebel yell routing the Federal infantry. We fought into the
night. Finally, the firing died out, and I received a Federal messenger to cease firing to allow the dead to be buried. We cooperated and gathered the wounded
and buried the dead in shallow graves. Hogs roamed the battleground consuming
the unburied.

Hill had removed himself from the ambulance to make an area to treat the
wounded. He resided in a tent under a nearby tree, and his report treated the gap
in his line as a minor vacancy. Since he was under my command I supported his
conclusion; however, Hill's performance thwarted his valiant performances at
Antietam. A battle lull allowed Hill to reignite the Hill-Jackson feud again, and

Hill continued to address his complaints to Lee. Finally, Lee turned the matter over to me since Hill served under my command. I advised Hill that the past actions were not a military issue, and Hill reacted by procuring legal advice forcing Lee to turn the matter over to headquarters in Richmond.

It had been a settling inactive winter, and the men kept warm and well fed. Lincoln had replaced Burnside with Gen. Hooker, and Hooker had restructured the Union army to attack Lee. He planned to catch Lee in crossfire between his Calvary and two segments of his army. Hooker's first action was to flank Lee with his calvary. He segmented the remaining army by leaving twenty-five percent stationary and marching with the major portion to Lee's left flank. It was obvious the Blue Bellies were ready for battle. Lee led his army to confront Hooker north of the Rapidan where it was the least likely place for a battle. Lee summoned his commanders together again at the crossroads of Chancellorsville to lay out the battle plans and bring us up to date on news from Pres. Davis. We met early morning in his headquarters. Outside, the bees were foraging among the spring blooms, and the birds were brightly singing. The air was clean and fresh among the trees. He began.

"Gentlemen, we began our first campaign for the year. First, I want to bring you up to date on the news from Richmond. Lincoln has declared the Emancipation Proclamation granting freedom to all slaves in Confederate States, and he was greatly supported by Greley Horiska, editor of the Post-Times. This recent move completely destroys any chance we have of gaining European support, and it also makes available the cheap labor, escaping slaves, for his war efforts. It increases the population of conscripts to serve in the Federal army. We may see fighting black troops before this war is over. This new act goes into effect after the first of the year. Now we must get on with the battle at hand."

Hill was the first to speak. "Gen. Lee, Hooker has pulled his army into the wilderness. I'll send a unit up Orange Turnpike for containment."

"Good move, Gen. Hill."

Hill immediately dispatched a unit to Orange Turnpike, and as the unit approached Chancellorsville they came under fire from the Federals. They took refuge in the woods, and we maintained our positions waiting further orders from Lee. Gen. Jeb Stuart had reported to Lee that Gen. Hooker had not fully deployed his troops. Hooker had deployed a unit on his right flank, which was without support. Lee made the decision to attack this Federal unit for maximum efficiency, and if he destroyed this unit, Hooker's army would be exposed. I was ordered to attack Hooker from the west with thirty thousand men. It was a twelve-mile march to get into position, and Hill's Light Brigade was to lead.

They were on time and marched double time followed by the remaining troops of the Stonewall Brigade. Hill's unit marched ten straight hours without rest. My army had made it on time, and after twelve hours from the start we were positioned directly on Hooker's flank. The Stonewall Brigade positioned itself in the wilderness in a one-mile radius, and the Light Brigade was held in reserve. I rode back to confer with Gen. Hill where I found him methodically organizing his troops. We rode into the woods together with a small contingency to determine Union activity. Our North Carolina troops were quite nervous hearing the Federal troops cutting trees to use for barricades.

Musket fire broke the silence, and return fire started a salvo. Hill indicated it was time to return to our unit, and it was well into night and difficult to determine who and where the enemy was. The officers' unit veered from the turnpike into the woods and made haste to their main unit. Hill rode ahead of the returning unit to advise the Carolinians we were returning. He was yelling for them to hold their fire at fifty yards from the main line.

One Carolinian yelled, "It's a trick. The woods are full of Federal Calvary. Let 'em have it."

At that time the Carolinians fired into the Hill-Jackson unit. The unit ceased to exist, and several Confederate soldiers and fourteen horses were immediately killed. I was shot in the arm and shoulder. Gen. Hill was immediately at my side, holding my head in his lap and cutting away my shirtsleeve to stop the bleeding. I drank brandy from his flask to diminish the pain. Gen. Hill related he would not make my condition known to the troops. I thanked him for that, and it was the last time I spoke with Gen. Hill. I was immediately treated by Hill's physician and transferred by ambulance to my own physician, Dr. McGuire. He performed a field amputation of my arm. I was transferred to the army hospital in Richmond where Elinor joined me during my recovery.

I was distraught from the loss of my left arm, but I would be able to return to the battlefield after recovery. We had many officers with amputated limbs serving the Confederate cause. I continued to carry the torch. Elinor continued to stay at my side each day. She had arranged for her brother's family to keep the children while she stayed with me. She told me how our children had grown, and that they attended school regularly. Tom was becoming a fine young man. The door opened and she came in.

"General, how are you today?"

"I'm doing well under the circumstances. My arm is better, and the hole in my shoulder is healing. My bandages were changed this morning, and I'll be able to return to my unit in a month or so if I continue to heal at this rate."

"You'll do no such thing if I have my say. You've done your war effort. You and John both have given everything, but your lives for this struggle."

"John who?"

"Didn't anyone tell you? Major Mosby occupies a room at the other end of the infirmary. He was shot during a Union raid at the Bishop's farm. He's been here recovering for months."

"When they let me out of this bed I'll go down and visit the old square rooter."

"He's in better shape than you are. I'll let him know you're here."

"Well, what are you waiting for? Hand me one of those lemons and go get him."

"Now Tom, you're so impatient. He may not be ready to visit you." She handed him the lemon. "Do you want me to peel it for you?"

"You know I eat these things with the peeling on."

She left to inquire about Mosby. Conversing with him would always cheer me up. She was gone only a short time when they returned together. Elinor entered the room first.

"Tom, he was as anxious to see you as you were to see him."

"What happened to you, Tom?"

"It's a long story. I did a dumb thing and paid the price. I was doing some reconnaissance before the Battle of Chancellorsville at dusk. The men were intense with all the activity around them, and we were surrounded by Union troops. Gen. Hill was riding outlook while we were returning through the woods. He rode hard toward our Carolina regiment shouting we were Confederates returning from scouting. The Carolina brigade thought it was a ploy, and the unit fired on the scouting party. I was shot twice. Other soldiers and horses were instantly killed. Dr. McGuire amputated my arm in the field and sent me here to recover. How are you doing?"

"I getting well and should be leaving anytime."

"I'm glad you doing better, John. I have one question for you."

"What's that, Tom?'

"Have you been doing any square rooting lately?" We both laughed. It had become a lifelong friendship ritual.

"Tom, I see you're still eating those lemons. I'll always be able to track you by lemon peels. It's good to see you again. I'll come by tomorrow and give you the news about Chancellorsville and other happenings I know about. There are many events occurring every day now."

He went around the bed and out the door leaving Elinor and me. I spent the remainder of the day with Elinor. Elinor and I were getting reacquainted again for the war had kept us apart. Here I lie in the bed shot up, and all we can do is hold hands; however, she's a delightful companion. I fell asleep earlier than usual. The sleep was filled with dreams. First, I dreamed of the children. Then I dreamed of plowing old Samantha and slopping the hogs. A nurse ready to change my bandages awakened me the next morning. Elinor had slept in a chair by the bed, and she began to stir when the nurse inquired.

"General, it's time to check your progress and change bandages." She began cutting away the bandages.

"How does it look?"

"It's healing. How do you feel?"

"I'm feeling better. Looks like Elinor's waking up."

"Dr. Hamilton will check you later." The nurse applied medication and new bandages, and she left the room.

"How do you feel, Tom?" Elinor inquired.

"I'm feeling better today than yesterday. Let's get some breakfast, and maybe I can spend some more time talking with John."

"We'll see if we can arrange that." She left the room to see about breakfast. She returned with breakfast, and afterwards she brought Mosby to the room.

"How are you today, Tom?"

"I'm doing better. Tell me what happened at Chancellorsville."

"Okay, General. You know we were greatly outnumbered by the Federals. After you were carried from the field the Stonewall Brigade was turned over to General Jeb Stuart. Union General Hooker for no reason abandoned Holly Grove Hill, and Stuart immediately put Confederate artillery in place. He bombarded Hooker's army at every opportunity. Gen. A. P. Hill was wounded shortly after you left the field, and the Light Brigade was given to Gen. Heth Hill. Heth led the infantry on many charges, almost breaking Hooker's lines. The Blue Bellies counterattacked with massive forces only to be driven back again. We finally routed Hooker, driving him back across the Rappahannock. During the route massive fires broke out at nightfall. The wounded on the battleground died in those fires. It was a victory but a costly one."

"Wish I could've been there, John. I would have loved to help make old Hooker run."

"I know you would Tom. You could do it too."

"Tell me more about your escapades, John. I hear all kinds of tales about you. Are they true?"

"Maybe, then again maybe they're just tales."

"Tell me why residents are calling you the Gray Ghost."

"Well, that may have come from a number of incidences. It could have been the time eight Confederate soldiers and I slipped into General Stroughton's camp and captured him while he slept in bed. It could be the time I almost captured Gen. Grant on his train at Manassas Junction. He was traveling on his private train with an escort of fifty men. I was thirty miles from there when I got the message he was arriving. I saddled up my three hundred raiders, and we made haste to the junction. We arrived too late to capture Hiram. Or it could be the care I take of the Virginia people. I protect them from Federal generals like Custer. He scares old ladies and hangs their sons."

"Gray Ghost, it seems like a fitting name."

"Whatever, I'm looking forward to getting back into action. In fact, I leave tomorrow for Winchester."

"I'll never forget our days at the Academy, John. I wonder if Sarge's still servicing O'Malley's nannies."

"We did have fun. We had a good time at Benny Havens Tavern too."

I spent two more hours with Mosby, reliving our younger days. It finally came time for him to leave. We shook hands and he turned leaving the room. It was the last time I saw the old square rooter. He was a true friend.

Elinor and I enjoyed dinner, and at times she stopped eating long enough to feed me. The dessert was the best part of the meal. She fed me that also. It was another restless night filled with dreams. The next morning Dr. Hamilton awakened me. He changed my bandages and checked my breathing.

"I hear fluid in your lungs. You have pneumonia. Continue your bed rest and apply a wet sponge to keep cool." He left the room and I fell asleep. Elinor was at my side. Again I dreamed of plowing and feeding the hogs. I dreamed Josh was helping me, and I was lost at the entry to the Academy. I dreamed until there were no more dreams. I realized I was no longer dreaming. At las...I get to cross over the river and rest under the tree.

My adult life was dedicated to the military, studying, learning and fighting wars. Early years were spent at hard work etching a farm living for the family. Then came my most enjoyable years at the Academy and making many new friends. Marrying the loves of my life and having my children, the most loved and important things in my life. It seems that my life's meaning was to fight wars. I lived thirty-nine years and most of that time I learned, taught and fought wars.

My life was about more than just fighting wars. It was about understanding the meaning of what causes the war. The Mexican War was simple to understand for it was simply fought for freedom. The War Between the States was a war fought with more difficult meanings. The meaning changed as the war progressed. However, I shall expose the real meaning and cause of that war. It was hidden in freedom from slavery. However, the real cause was economics, greed and power, and I have unravel that scheme.

It took a few days to adjust to my new circumstances and surroundings. I didn't know where I was, but it didn't matter. I could tune in on things and happenings for my ghost was amazing. I could be any place at anytime just by thinking about it. I could watch Elinor and the children laugh and play. My demise was difficult for them to accept in the beginning, but they grew to accept it.

It was July 1. Lee was beginning to make his biggest blunder, and my ghost accompanied him. He decided to go on the offensive and attack the north. He assembled his reorganized army at Cashtown, Pennsylvania. The plan was to have Hill take charge of General Pender's brigade to lead the attack at Gettysburg. William Pegram's Confederate artillery was efficiently positioned at Gettysburg, and gunners exchanged fire all morning with the entrenched Federals. At noon, Pender's infantry charged directly at the Federal's artillery, and his infantry suffered great losses. Union infantry's first line broke, and the Confederates continued the attack making advances on the second line. The second line was beginning to buckle when reserved artillery opened its deadly fuselage. The Confederate soldiers were almost out of ammunition, and nightfall came when Hill withdrew his men.

Lee sent orders to Gen. Ewell to attack and occupy Cemetery Ridge; however, slow communication and Gen. Ewell's reaction time negated Lee's command. Gen. Meade became well entrenched on Cemetery Ridge. The second day was a continuation of the first, attacking the massive Federal army. There were continuous advances and withdrawals until nightfall. Night fell with a continuous and needless exchange of artillery fire. No one could see the enemy to direct the firing, and finally the firing ceased. The third day began with the usual artillery exchange. The smell of sulfur and death engulfed the battleground. Again, Hill ordered Pender's men forward to take Cemetery Ridge, and Union artillery fire gutted Confederate lines as they advanced. Heroic efforts were in vain as Confederate troops made advances on the entrenched Federals. I stood next to Lee and Hill throughout the battle, and often I advised them. I knew the enemy and where their weaknesses were. I pleaded but they could not hear me, and it could have been my greatest contribution to the war. Finally, nightfall closed the third day of war at Gettysburg, and Lee withdrew the Army of Northern Virginia back to Virginia.

I turned my attention to Washington, and it was easy in my new state. All I had to do was think where I wanted to be and I was there. Lincoln had moved Grant into Washington to confer with him often. He and Julia occupied a small brick house in the center of town. One day Grant was visiting the president in the Whitehouse, and I could hear him talking with Lincoln.

"Mr. President, we cannot deal with the rebels by occupying Richmond. We must occupy the entire south, and I need more experienced officers to defeat southerners in the larger cities. I would like to nominate William T. Sherman as one of those officers. He can march through Chattanooga into Georgia and take Atlanta."

"Gen. Grant, I think you're right. Once we take Atlanta, it's a matter of chasing down other Confederate officers and defeating their armies. Gen. Meade has Lee occupied in Virginia, and it's only a matter of time. We cannot delay defeating the South too long especially if enough time remains for another election before the war ends. The democrats will pursue peace you know, and we cannot have peace without unifying this country."

"Thank you, sir. I'll contact Gen. Sherman and set the plan in motion."

If I could only get this news to Lee and Davis, the war is almost over with these plans. The south is running out of supplies and support, and it does not have the financial backing nor the industrial might to continue fighting. From hereon we'll be on the run awaiting the final battle for we lost the conflict three battles ago.

I returned to the mountains of Virginia to see the children start the school year. Elinor and the children were going on with their lives. Elinor was still young, and our families would raise the children.

Again, I returned to Washington. Hiram had summoned Gen. Sherman to his office.

"Sherm, we must conquer the south. First, you must take Chattanooga then march to Atlanta. You'll have everything you need. You will be provided troops, rations, artillery, horses and ammunitions, and if you run out, we'll give you more. You are to burn Atlanta, and we'll rebuild it once the war is over. Do you understand?"

"Yes, Sir."

Gen. Sherman saluted and left Grant's office to assume command of his army. He followed Hiram's orders completely. His army won the Battle of Chattanooga, and he marched south burning Atlanta. Sherman's actions allowed Grant to occupy Richmond and to subdue the strong will of the southerners. It was obvious Sherman's advances in the South worried Lee. Lee could no longer divide his army to create diversions. He was busy surviving with his ragtag troops, and he could only stall Grant and Meade's' occupation of Richmond. I tried to get a message to Lee but found it impossible. My new state allowed me to be any place at anytime I wanted. However, as an immortal I could not communicate with mortals. I could have given so much information to Lee so he could formulate battle plans. My all-knowing position leaves me with one conclusion, and that was the Confederates could not win this struggle. I must find my friend Hill again for he requires watching over.

Gen. Hill was marching his defeated army south from Gettysburg in a horrendous rainfall. Union Gen. George Custer pursued the Confederates to Mill Creek, Virginia. Gen. Hill grew tired of Custer's nuisance at his rear. He turned his army and dispersed Custer's brigade, and he continued marching his army to Orange. After resting his army, Lee ordered Hill to move against Meade's Federals at Briscoe Station. In spite of a recent bout with prostatitis Hill quickly marched against the Blue Bellies. He moved his artillery onto the hills overlooking Briscoe Station, and his artillery commander immediately caught the Union army in crossfire, routing them in a northerly direction. The Confederates pursued the fleeing Union army to be confronted by three entrenched Union divisions, and Hill's brigade took direct deadly musket fire. The Federals were enclosing on the rear of the Confederate charge preventing retreat. Realizing the situation, the Confederates charged forward again breaking the Union line only to be met by a second color bearer line. More volleys from the second Union division initiated an unorganized hasty retreat. Confederates rushed by supporting troops and artillery, and the artillerymen joined the retreat leaving the cannons for the Federals. The Federals rolled the cannons down the hill, and they added them to their artillery unit. Hill guided the Confederates back to Orange. It was Hill's most devastating loss, and he questioned his ability to lead a large army. Lee gave Hill's unit time to regroup in Orange before ordering him to Parker's Store along Orange Turnpike. Hill's unit and the Confederates maintained a defensive posture until Appomattox.

Hill proceeded along Orange Turnpike to the Trapp Farm, which afforded a good view of the nearby turnpike and Federal troops to the north. He immediately placed his artillery at an elevated clearing in a surrounding area, which had become known as the Wilderness. Union troops came out of the woods, muskets blazing, and Hill's unit returned the fire driving them back into the trees. This was the beginning of a battle at Brock Road. After the Union troops retreated to the woods Confederate soldiers followed with muskets blazing, only to be repulsed by the Blue Bellies second line of defense. The Confederates fell back in defensive positions, and Federals went on the offensive suffering great losses. Night fell and the Union army dug in, and the dead laid on the battleground.

Confederate lines were in disarray for the men were tired after two days of marching and fighting. The air was filled with the smell of sulfur from the artillery and musket fire, and Hill rose early the next day suffering from pain in his lower back. His leftmost line needed to be reinforced, and he lacked manpower for reinforcement. If the Federals concentrated an attack there, his line would definitely give way. Grant began an infantry attack early the next morning with Union troops advancing on the defensive Confederates at Trapp's farm. The advancement cost them great losses, but they continued to attack. Grant was using green conscript troops from Pennsylvania, and his attack continued throughout the day. The Confederates were routed until Gen. Longstreet appeared turning the tide of the attack. Longstreet combined his army with Hill's, and they drove the Federals back across Brock Road. Hill's ultimate desire was to reunite with Gen. Ewell. The battle was halted again at nightfall; however, the third day it again started early. Soldiers from both sides were too exhausted to fight a third day. During the charge to regain the Trapp farm Gen. Longstreet was shot through the neck by friendly fire, and he collapsed and died within hours. From the clearing Lee and Hill could see Federal artillery moving in the direction of Spotsylvania.

Hill's condition had worsened, and he asked Lee to be replaced. Prostatitis had rendered him unfit for battle forcing Lee to assign the inexperienced Gen. Early as his replacement. Hill converted an ambulance into a mobile bed to follow Lee and his army to Spotsylvania. Lee beat Grant to Spotsylvania and procured the advantage defensive position.

Grant's color guard led the attack and Lee responded by defending his earthworks. He ordered Gen. Heth Hill to counterattack Grant's left flank, and the battle raged for two days. The third day it was obvious Grant's plans were to conquer the Confederates. He ordered wave after wave of Union troops and artillery at the earthworks. It was twenty solid hours of fighting and destruction, and the weather changed and the rain started to fall. The dead and dying lay in the battlefield with raindrops washing blood from the wounds into the trenches. After ten days of fighting Grant again moved his army southeast, and Lee had no choice but to follow and defend railroads leading to Richmond. Gen. Hill recovered from his illness in time to command his unit in the Battle of Cold Harbor, and

Cold Harbor was a mistake for Grant. His attacks cost the Blue Bellies more losses. Finally, having no success he withdrew his troops in the direction of the James River, settling at Petersburg. Petersburg is located twenty miles south of Richmond, and Grant's ambition was to occupy Richmond. If he took Petersburg, Richmond would be easy to invade. Again Lee would have no choice but to follow, and Lee ordered Hill to follow the Union troops.

He immediately encountered skirmishes at Malvern Hill, which lasted throughout the day. Hill was forced to battle with Federal calvary. Confederate forces lacked calvary support to follow Grant's march, making Hill's action all that more important. Hill's unit continued to follow Grant, positioning his army between Richmond and Petersburg. Gen. Hill marched his army toward Petersburg, and Grant was making Petersburg's outskirts the location for his headquarters. Hill arrived in Petersburg to find Gen. Beauregard barely hanging on to maintain control of the area. Hill knew the Federals had overwhelming manpower and position. He was determined to support the cause if he could maintain his health. Federal siege of Petersburg went on for eight months with attacks and counterattacks. Finally, a western Pennsylvania unit persuaded Grant to mine underneath the Confederates and plant explosives. I was unable to warn Gen. Hill; however, the Confederates suspected a mining operation sank four thirty-foot shafts trying to locate the mining shafts. The Federals loaded the end of their shaft with two thousand pounds of gunpowder, and placed sandbags over one end of the charge to direct the blast directly toward the Confederate lines. Union mining engineers spliced fuses and set off the gunpowder charge one late July evening. The blast took out four Confederate Artillery pieces and killed and wounded four hundred infantrymen.

A large pit erupted in the middle of the Confederate front line, and Union troops rushed forth into the gigantic pit. A second Union line rushed into the pit, and they appeared to loose direction and leadership. It was as if they were overcome by the curiosity of the hole. Meanwhile, the Confederates regained composure, and they rushed upon the Union troops firing muskets and using bayonets. The battle continued until there was a mass of soldiers partially filling the pit. After another twenty hours of battle, Grant pulled his army back and devised a new strategy. He moved his troops to encircle the Confederates for his plan to advance through the mining explosion was a failure. Grant's frontal assault failed to achieve the objective, and Hill had defeated Grant again.

Grant continued the siege of Petersburg with attacks and bombardments. There were continuous talks by Federal leadership of evading Richmond and Petersburg. The Federals made some success by attacking Fort Harrison at Richmond, and the success forced Lee to move troops from Petersburg to Richmond. Grant separated forty thousand of his massive army to Hill's flank; however, it was a mismanaged affair from the beginning. Hill sent his cavalry against the Union army, and the Blue Bellies were forced to leave the field after suffering many deaths.

Gen. Hill's prostate condition worsened by spreading to his kidney and urinary tract. However, he continued to lead his men through the winter. The Confederates were without shoes, coats and blankets during this cold winter weather, and food was practically nonexistent. The main staples were turnips and potatoes, and these staples were prepared every way imaginable. Many Confederates deserted to rejoin their families for many of them realized they were supporting a losing effort.

It was the middle of spring and Grant's continuous attacks and bombardments were taking their toll on Petersburg. He was in the process of delivering the knockout blow to end the war. Hill mounted his horse with two couriers at his side, and his ever-present illness made it almost impossible for him to ride. However, his mind was on the military strategy at hand. He peered through his telescope across the clearing to view Union troops breaking Confederate lines on the right. They were backed by heavy artillery fire; however, they were unorganized in their victory march. Hill immediately noticed Poague's artillery was silent, and he rode toward that position to make his artillery engage the enemy. The couriers were maintaining pace with Hill when they came upon two Union infantrymen. The couriers came down on the infantrymen with drawn revolvers and the Union soldiers immediately surrendered. Gen. Hill ordered one of the couriers to take the prisoners to the rear, and he and the other courier continued down Boydton Road toward the artillery. Suddenly, the courier spotted two more Federal soldiers in the woods behind a large tree with muskets pointed in their directions. Gen. Hill rode toward the two Federal troops demanding them to surrender. Two shots rang out, and Gen. Hill lunged from the saddle.

He lived only a few minutes after he hit the ground, and I was holding his head when he died. He never uttered a word. Little Powell had crossed over the river to rest under the tree with me. He was a valiant soldier and leader, and like me he was born to practicing war. His entire life had been in preparation for this moment. He had suffered greatly, performing his duty in the war enduring one indiscretion in his life. Confederate infantry captured the two Federal soldiers and moved Hill's body to the rear. He was transported in an army wagon with his cape covering his face. He was buried in Richmond's Hollywood Cemetery. After Davis's death he would be interred in the same cemetery near Hill.

Lee began the march with the remaining Confederate army toward Appomattox, and Grant continued to keep the Confederate army busy with attacks. He suffered great losses, but the Union efforts kept Lee from turning attention to Gen. Sherman's actions in Atlanta. Gen. Sherman's Federals defeated Confederate Gen. John Hood meeting little resistance. He marched into city hall in Atlanta, and he raised the Stars and Stripes in Georgia's capital. Hood retreated a few miles south of Atlanta. Grant immediately arranged a meeting with Gen. Sherman in Shenandoah Valley to celebrate the victory. Grant's first action when he met Sherman was to throw his hat into the air. After the meeting he returned to Petersburg, and he gave Sherman a one hundred cannon salute. The cannons were also aimed at the Confederates, and Grant ordered Sherman to march across Georgia to defeat Confederate Gen. Joe Johnston.

In the meantime the national election pitted Lincoln against former Union Gen. McClellan, and Lincoln won almost as if he were unopposed. Grant, Sherman and Sheridan's victories contributed greatly to Lincoln's reelection.

After Sherman burned Atlanta, he marched to Savannah burning everything in his path, and he conquered Savannah with little resistance. After Savannah he turned his sight on Columbia, South Carolina, and a month later Columbia was added to Sherman's conquered list. These victories led Davis and Lee to peace considerations. I sadly watched as the Stars and Bars were lowered at each battle. Lee and Davis had many discussions about peace negotiations, and Gen. Lee finally explained to Davis the only terms Grant and Lincoln would accept was the return of the Confederate states back to the Union. Gen. Lee initiated peace negotiations. He sent an officer under a flag of truce to open a discussion for a peace settlement, and Grant informed Lee that he was not authorized to negotiate peace. He would require the president's permission. Grant returned his compliments, and advised Lee that he wanted to keep communications open.

Both Petersburg and Richmond were now in Federal hands, and the Confederate capital was moved to Danville, Virginia. The Army of Northern Virginia remained intact but without food. Lee raced south to find food at Appomattox, Virginia and to unite his army with Johnston's. Sheridan's calvary cut Lee off at Appomattox Court House.

Grant joined Sheridan's calvary, sending a courier to Lee recommending surrender, and Lee agreed to Grant's recommendations with terms. After a sleepless night Lee found Grant's term was southern troops would not take up arms against the Union, and the surrender at Appomattox instituted the surrender of all Confederate generals. One exception to the surrender was the Gray Ghost, Col. John Singleton Mosby (The Old Square Rooter). He dissolved into thin air;

however, he always drew a crowd years after the war. Anytime he appeared in any southern town square he was immediately surrounded by loving followers.

Lee struggled after the war until he procured the position of Washington University president. Later the university was to be renamed Washington and Lee University to honor him. He ran the school much as he did his army. On October 10, 1870, he gave his last order, "Strike the tents." He closed his eyes and crossed over the river to rest under the tree.

CHAPTER 5

▼

THE AFTERMATH

I could no longer accept the happenings of war, and I wanted to walk by the river at the Academy. Sure enough I was there, and I waded into the water remembering the times when we all swam together. It was difficult to believe national development brought us to so much adversity. The country had changed, and we needed to change the nations labor force to areas of the country where there would be more economical development. The northern industrial growth and development required that greater labor force. The southern states could only grow cotton and food, and both could be imported at a minimal cost. The rest of the world needed the products of the northern mills, which would give us great economic influence. The next stop was the mess hall and Jefferson Hall, and I sat on the porch of our quarters remembering the tobacco episode. I strolled down to the stable, not finding Little Sorrell. Old Sarge had been replaced with a younger descendant. O'Malley's farm had been bought and replaced with Academy dormitories.

I walked to Benny Havens Tavern to find it had been replaced with a dry good store. I stood in front of the new building, and my thoughts returned to Mary Morrison. I walked into the woods where we shared many passionate hours. I wanted to visit Roses on Church Street one more time to see if the colonel and Rosemary were still there. It was early evening, and I entered Roses and stood near the sofa. Two men were waiting their turn for the evening's adventure. At that moment Rosemary appeared at the top of the stairs.

"Mr. Greley Horiska and Mr. Andrew Milton, how are you this fine evening? Are you ready for an evening of fun and entertainment? Mr. Horiska, I've saved Sweet Sarah Lee for you, and for you Andrew I have a long-legged brunette. How does that suit your fancy?"

"Well Madam, bring Sweet Sarah on down, and let's get on with the party." demanded Greley.

Rosemary disappeared upstairs to fetch the girls as Greley turned to Andrew.

"You know, Andy, our plan is unfolding. I'd estimate it's about half revealed."

"What do you mean, half revealed?

"Andrew, do you mean to tell me that you've been a member of the first political machine in this country started in 1860, and you don't know what's been going on?"

"Now, Horiska, I know there's been a war, and I'm glad it's over."

"You don't remember what this war was all about? In 1860, we had meetings at the Post-Times Building where we formulated the economic pattern for this country for the next hundred years? This pattern restructured the nation's economy to make it a leader in the world economy. The nation's government policies changed to support the developing industries. These changes led to revolt and a war. The projection was our nation should be the world's economic leader, and we needed the labor force for our industrial complex. The south wasn't using the labor efficiently. Their representatives were keeping the labor force down on the farm, and we needed to develop our manufacturing base. The labor force freed from the south will be better utilized, and they will be paid for their labor. Of course it'll cost them more to live. They'll be paid in inflated dollars, and they'll be working so hard that it'll take them a hundred years to figure out that they've only been moved from one place to another. By that time these issues will be problems for someone else."

"Greley, you mean we fought the War Between the States over economics?

"Yes. Now we must efficiently tidy the mess and get on with business."

"What's the mess?"

"It's the aftermath ridding the nation of Lincoln, Johnson and Davis. The rest will politically take care of itself. Lincoln is getting ready to spend millions on reconstructing the south. The south can take care of itself."

Rosemary appeared at the top of the stairs with Sweet Sarah and the long-legged brunette.

"Well, gentlemen, are you ready?"

They didn't wait for Rosemary to proceed down the stairs. Greley was the first upstairs, and he grabbed Sweet Sarah by the hand disappearing in the nearest

room. Andrew was more hesitant allowing Rosemary to performed a brief introduction, and they walked to a nearby room. It had been an interesting conversation, and I remained at Roses and watched the comings and goings. In my state
no one would ever know, and I was getting used to being a ghost and liked it. If
only I could communicate with mortals. I waited one hour and Greley was the
first to come down stairs. Sweet Sarah gave him a hug at the top of the stairs, and
he rewarded her handsomely. Andrew followed shortly, joining Greley on the
sofa.

After a short humorous conversation they proceeded to their carriage, and we
boarded. Greley turned to Andrew in a humorous manner.

"Well, Andrew, did you get your money's worth?"

"I reckon. Greley, I'm glad you brought me to this place. We've enjoyed some
good times here."

"We'll come again sometimes. First, we must attend to important reconstruction business. The Post-Times Building is the meeting place to continue the
reconstruction saga. Andrew, you must be there at nine o'clock in the morning.
We must continue the meeting we started in 1860. From now on I'll expect you
to remember everything for it's important. You can't go around forgetting our
mission. Tomorrow you will meet Mary Surratt and Capt. John Wilkes Booth, a
Confederate officer."

"But Greley, the war is over." Andrew exclaimed.

"Andy, our mission is only half over."

It had become very interesting, and I would be at the Post-Times Building at
nine o'clock. After all, who could stop me? I was in the Post-Times boardroom
the nest day when the meeting begin. Other attendees were Mary Surratt, John
Boothe, Andrew Milton and Greley Horiska. The meeting was informal, and it
began casually with Andrew posing a question.

"Where is the rest of the political machine you talked about last night?"

"Andrew, it's all here. You must always know the paper has great national
influence."

Andrew looked at Greley questioningly as Greley began explaining the main
purpose of the meeting.

"Do we need any introductions? If not, we'll get on with the meeting. Miss
Mary and Capt. Boothe, you know the reason we've gathered here. We must
change government thinking concerning reconstruction, and the most efficient
method to change it is to eliminate the top people."

Boothe spoke, "Sir, I would like to continue the fight to liberate the South."

"John, that's a useless fight. You follow my advice, and you'll be rewarded handsomely. There'll be money and opportunity aplenty, and you'll find a way to achieve southern influence. We must develop a plan to eliminate the president and vice president in order to diminish the reconstruction expenditure."

Mary spoke up. "We'll take care of the details. We see Lincoln and Johnson almost every day. We'll become part of their social circle, and the next thing you know the nation will have a new president and vice president."

"What's the time frame for these occurrences?"

"Six months, maybe nine."

"Well, it's an initial plan. They've captured Davis down in Georgia, and we'll have to see what they're going to do with him. You know Lincoln and Davis are two ordinary old Kentucky boys, and Johnson isn't any better. He's a mountain klutz from east Tennessee. If the south hadn't seceded from the Union these leaders would never have made the necessary economic changes. It's almost unbelievable they were elected to leading governmental positions; however, it simplified the overall process. Let's get on with your plan, Mary."

"Tomorrow, Capt. Boothe and I will return to Washington, and my boarding house will serve as our headquarters. We'll report the details as plans are developed."

"Meanwhile, Andy and I shall keep an eye on Jeff Davis."

I accompanied Mary and John on the boring train trip back to Washington. We embarked from the train late that night and went straight to the boarding house. I decided to become a boardinghouse resident until plans were developed. The next day a planning meeting was held in Boothe's room. Mary, John, Edwin Boothe and Hannibal Surratt, Mary's husband, attended the meeting. John initiated the dialogue.

"I've thought the plan through. We'll all have to take chances and suffer any consequences if we're caught. I'll be responsible for assassinating Lincoln. Edwin, you'll have to take care of Secretary Stewart, and Hannibal, Johnson is yours. Lincoln always attends premiers at the Ford Theater, and later this month I open a premier called <u>My American Cousin</u>. Lincoln and Mary will be in the president's balcony seats, and I'll take care of him there prior to the performance. We'll have to gather more information on Johnson and Stewart to plan their demise."

They continued to meet evening after evening until the premier at Ford Theater. It was finally decided that Edwin would knife Stewart on his stroll home after work, and Johnson would meet his demise by a gunshot from Hannibal while dining at his favorite restaurant in Washington. On the day of the premier at Ford Theater I decided to visit Lincoln in the White House. I arrived in time for tea in the living room. The Lincolns were entertaining the Grants. Mary was wearing her latest low cut evening attire. Her dress was excessively low cut compared to dress styling. I didn't mind if Abe didn't mind. She began the conversation.

"Why General Grant, you did a marvelous job performing your duty defeating the Confederate Army."

"Thank you, Mrs. Lincoln. I was only serving my country."

"How modest you are, General. Please call me Mary. Julia, did you miss your handsome husband while he was away at war?"

"Of course. I stayed home in Missouri with my folks, and Hiram would visit me when the military could spare him."

"Hiram? General Grant I didn't know your name was Hiram."

"It's a long story. I would rather enjoy the tea than talk about me when I was Hiram."

It was obvious the Grants were uncomfortable with the small talk when the president interceded. Julia was uncomfortable with the way Mary was coming onto Hiram.

"Now Miss Mary, we mustn't be so forward. The Grants are probably anxious to be on their way to the hotel. They have a train to catch later tonight, and they must pack to leave."

Lincoln summoned the carriage and walked with Hiram to the door.

"Gen. Grant, you did a good job defeating the Confederate Army. And I shall never forget your magnificent efforts. You mustn't mind my Mary. She's the center entertainment here in Washington."

The carriage arrived, and Mary and Julia had caught up with the men at the door. It was a cold parting between Julia and Mary, and the general and the president each raised an eyebrow as they parted.

I returned to the boarding house to remain until the theater opened. I was the first inside the theater, and I positioned myself in the rear of the presidential balcony. The theater was beginning to fill to capacity. The president and first lady were seated front row center in the balcony. Just minutes before the play was to begin John Boothe entered the presidential balcony, and he shot Lincoln in the back of the head with his derringer. He immediately jumped from the balcony to the stage floor, and the jump broke his leg when he landed. The audience applauded for they thought the play had begun. John dragged himself from the stage out the side door to a waiting horse. I went along with John, and we galloped along the main road passing a carriage. We paused long enough to identify

Hiram and Julia Grant as the occupants. John galloped away through the countryside until the pain in his leg became unbearable, and he took shelter in a barn.

I returned to the boarding house to find Mary there with Hannibal and Edwin. Edwin had performed his task but Hannibal lacked the courage and changed his mind at the last minute. The next day the Post-Times headlines read "President Assassinated." The president died at a house across from Ford Theatre in the morning hours, and the assassin was killed in a barn outside Washington. The article went on to relate that Secretary Stewart had been knifed. Andrew Johnson was sworn in as president early that day.

I returned to Rosemary's in New York to view the actions of Greley Horiska and Andrew Milton. It wasn't boring being a resident at Rosie's. Every important man in the city came by at least once a week. The following Saturday evening Greley and Andrew came into the parlor and took their usual seat on the sofa. They were alone in the parlor, and Greley turned to Andrew.

"Well Andy, how does it feel to be part of this machine?"

"It's great, Greley. Wish I understood more about it and how it works."

"It just works. Johnson was sworn in as president. The south hates him, and the north doesn't trust him. He'll be so busy developing his policies he won't have time to realize what going on in this country. By the time he figures out how to run the country he'll be out of office, and Grant will be elected president. Grant will be no better than Johnson as president; however, it'll allow us enough time to establish this world controlling economic machine we've already started. Grant is a military man, and he knows nothing about running the country's business. The people will elect him because he's a war hero. It'll take the south at least a hundred years to recover. The slaves will also struggle during that same time period. They'll make good laborers in the factories. We have to get on with this country's development. Speaking of getting on, here comes Rosie now."

"Hello, Mr. Horiska. How are you this evening? We haven't seen you around much lately."

"I'm fine, Miss Rosie."

"Who's your pleasure tonight?"

"I'll take Sweet Sarah."

"It just so happens Miss Sarah is available, and she is one of the more popular ones. The cadets from the Academy love her for she's made men out many of those first time cadets." They all laughed as she departed to get Sarah. She returned with Sarah, and Greley and Sarah disappeared. Rosie turned to Andrew.

"I hope he takes longer than fifteen minutes this time. Now, Mr. Milton, who's your pleasure?" She summoned the next available girl, and Andrew went upstairs for an evening of pleasure.

I continued to reside in New York and Washington. The Post-Times published articles supporting freeing Jefferson Davis, and it emphasized the lessons learned from the war and gave him partial credit. The editor paid fifty thousand dollars and finally Davis was pardoned to live in exile at Gulfport, Mississippi. The newspaper explained he would no longer be a threat to the country. The war had run its course and the accomplishments would be measured in the future. Davis returned to Mississippi, and he built his mansion in Gulfport from the gold he squirreled away while raising money for the Confederate cause. He lived there writing his memoirs and died in 1889.

Meanwhile, Johnson continued struggling trying to run the country, and the senate opposed all his programs. They even tried to impeach him before he completed the presidential term. Election Day finally put him out of his misery. As the machine predicted Grant defeated Johnson for the presidency. The Post-Times supplied campaign advertisements for him during his bid. Johnson refused to attend the presidential inauguration ceremony. In the ceremony Grant recognized the reconstruction program; however, he was so naïve during his tenure in office that very little was done toward reconstruction. Hiram was in awe of business and rich men. He was too easily swayed, and he was not a good judge of character when it came to spending federal monies. Appomattox had made him president. Since he was a war hero all he had to do was to throw his hat into the ring. The next thing he knew he was taking the oath of office. He appointed Rawlins as Secretary of War, Parker was made head of Indian Affairs and his buddy, Sherm, was his army general. Custer remained the youngest general in his army.

Hiram could run the military, but he didn't understand national economics. The administration advised him to buy gold for the national treasury when he had been trying to sell gold. He struggled trying to keep tabs on the White House, and Julia was moving relatives in daily. There were days when he returned home that he didn't know which bedroom he was supposed to sleep in. Company presidents convinced him that everything he did was for the American working man. Between the congressional bills and farmers complaining about not enough cash for their crops it was good news for Hiram when the Sioux went on a rampage in the Black Hills. Parker went into his office one day to announce that settlers were moving into the Black Hills when gold was discovered on the Indian reservation there.

"Mr. President, Sitting Bull and the Sioux nation is going on the warpath against the settlers intruding in the Black Hills."

"Parker, I've got a cure for Sitting Bull. I'll send Gen. Custer to deal with him. Only a year ago I was paying settlement fees to the Indians for peace. Now, here we are ready to deal with these people again. Custer is interested in becoming president, and he would see this challenge as an opportunity to be elected."

The next day Gen. Custer and John Mosby were sitting together in the waiting room outside Hiram's office. The president sent his secretary to fetch Mosby.

"Mr. Mosby, the president will see you now."

"Thank you." He followed her into Hiram's office.

"Mr. President, thank you for seeing me."

"Well, John. I've wanted to meet you ever since I got the letter from you concerning Gen. Custer hanging some of your troops. You know that was a straightforward letter, and it showed honor and courage. I respect that. Have you and your buddy been having a good visit in the waiting room?"

"Custer's act was not defined in the articles of war. Our soldiers were not criminals, and they should not have been hanged. Our visit was short and awkward. I came at your request to serve our country in China."

"Yes, I need a good man to serve as ambassador to China. Are you interested?"

"Certainly, sir."

"The job is yours. You'll leave next month with you wife and family members. The appointment is the least I can do for you. After all, it was your support in the south during the last election which got me elected."

"Thank you, sir."

"Mosby, do us a good job. Now, I must assign Custer the task of putting the Sioux Indians back in line in the Black Hills. They've been attacking the settlers who are trying to mine some of their gold."

"I shall do my best in China, and I wish you good luck with the Indians." Mosby exited the president's office as his secretary invited Gen. Custer to receive his assignment.

Gen. G. A. Custer was assigned to take three hundred troops to the Black Hills to quiet the Sioux Indian uprising. Hiram made a mistake for he left dealing with the Sioux Indians entirely to Custer. He had forgotten Custer was the bottom of our class, and he didn't give him specific orders. Gen. Custer outfitted his troops, boarded the train and headed straight for the Black Hills. I went along for the adventure. He and his officers made battle plans on the way. Upon reaching the Black Hills they camped and organized for two weeks. Custer grew tired of having his troops camping and practicing the Indian attack, and he started for

Little Bighorn to meet Gen. Terry a day early. His battle plan was to route the Sioux by surprise, starting at one end of their camp and riding roughshod through it. He misread his maps of the Sioux encampment, and he rode into the middle of ten thousand Indians. The Sioux surrounded the Seventh Calvary and the massacre began. Sitting Bull repeatedly attacked, inflicting great losses on the soldiers. Finally, Custer and two lieutenants were the only three remaining fighting the massive Sioux nation. Custer went down, followed by the lieutenants. Custer's scalp was removed to find its resting-place at Sitting Bull's totem pole. Gen. Custer crossed over the Little Bighorn River and rested on the other side. He was a daring general to the end.

Returning to Washington I was privilege to Hiram and Sherman's conversation. Sherman was seeking Grant's permission to put down the Sioux uprising. Grant related to Sherm that he was tired of the whole presidency mess.

"Look, Sherm, Custer mishandled the entire affair. He was using this Indian War to get elected president after my term is over. He was always a poor soldier, and we always assigned him minor task during the war. He could never lead more than a thousand men at a time. He wasn't even able to follow orders to meet with Gen. Terry."

"We can't leave those Indians unpunished, or they'll be attacking every settler within a hundred mile radius."

"You take care of it, Sherm. I have to persuade congress to give Pres. Lincoln's widow an annual stipend to live on. It seems she was declared insane a few years ago and she is without income. I'd be insane too if I had nothing to live on. Recently, the court judged her to be sane again. I guess she got smarter as she got older. Greley Horiska doesn't get financial support for former First Ladies. He only supports the former Confederate president. Sherm, I'm going to take a trip. I'm tired of being president."

Sherman prepared the program to defeat the Sioux Nation, and President Grant's term ended. He and Julia set out to see the world.

Mary Todd Lincoln was happy for she could enjoy a meager living and keep her sanity. The Grants visited England, France, Spain, India and China before returning home. They were greeted royally, and Hiram was hailed more as a general than a president. Mosby took a skiff out to receive the Grants when it anchored in Hong Kong harbor.

"Greetings, Mr. President and Mrs. Grant." He stuck out his hand to shake the president's.

"Greetings to you, Mr. Mosby. I see you're still a federal government employee."

"Ah pshaw, if it hadn't been for you I wouldn't be a federal employee. I never thought I would see the day when I was employed by the federal government and you weren't."

"Yes, my job finally ran out and not a bit too soon. Had I known the presidency job was going to be so demanding and difficult, Lee and I would still be at Appomattox discussing surrender. After all it was Appomattox that put me in the presidency."

"Oh hush." Julia interceded as Mosby put out his hand to aid her onto the skiff.

Mosby ferried them into China for three days of dining and entertaining. After the third day he ferried them back to the ship never to see Hiram again. The Grants left China and returned home. Upon arriving, Hiram found himself a civilian and broke again. Commodores Vanderbilt purchased the Grants a nice home near the Hudson River in New York City, and he started Hiram a brokerage business, which became defunct after two years of operation. Hiram's health was showing signs of failure, and he worried about Julia and his family's existence after his demise. In 1884 Hiram begin writing his memoirs, and he completed them exactly one year later. It was his only success in civilian life. Like me, he was always trained to perform military work. A week after he completed his memoirs, the boy I met on the train my first trip to the Academy died. He went down to the banks of the Hudson River and there rested in peace.

Mosby returned home to Washington, and President Hayes appointed him to be a Department of Justice official. He served this post for twenty years, then he returned to his civilian law practice. The practice cost him more money than he made, forcing him to close the doors. However, he continued to live in Washington. Greley Horiska's son, Thomas, learned of Mosby's existence in Washington and searched him out for an interview. Thomas could always recognize a good story. He had located the Confederate Gray Ghost, and he approached the Mosby resident in an average Washington neighborhood on August 1, 1914 finding Mosby sitting on the front porch barefooted and in his bathrobe.

"Mr. Mosby, I'm Thomas Greley from The Post-Times, and I came to interview you. I would like to capture some of your remarks about the War Between the States."

"Welcome, you must be Greley's son. You're too young to be Greley. I'll be happy to tell you everything you want to know. You know it was good of your pappy to get Jefferson Davis set free. I want to thank you for that."

"Dad always tried to do the best for this country. He died five years ago. He always said there were many inventions, which came from the war. He said it was amazing at the change in military tactics and advances in artillery as a result of the war."

"I'm sure there was much to be learned from the war; however, it was terrible so many lives were lost to learn a valuable lesson. It's a lesson we must never repeat. Let me have the Missus make you a cup of tea."

"Thank you very much."

"Mrs. Mosby, would you make Thomas a cup of tea?"

"Sure, John. I'll be a few minutes."

"Okay, John. Tell me the main incident that earned you the name of Gray Ghost."

"Ah pshaw, Thomas. If it were any one particular thing, it would have to be the time I slipped into the Federal Headquarters at Fairfax Courthouse and captured Gen. Ed Stoughton. We traded him for fifty Confederate prisoners. It was a dark rainy night, and I slipped into Stoughton's camp. I moved quietly by the posted guards. The night was so dark and rainy the federal guards thought I was a federal soldier returning to headquarters. I walked by the guard and made my way to the general's quarters. I knocked on the door as if I had been invited. His guard opened the door expecting another Union soldier, and I quickly overpowered the guard and marched into the general's bedchamber. I sat on his bed, and he remained sound asleep. I finally had to wake him.

"Who's there?" he asked.

"Mosby." I replied.

"That no good son of a bitch has been causing me all kinds of problems. Send troops to capture him and bring him to me." The general stated.

"You don't understand, general. You're my prisoner. You see sir. I'm John Mosby."

"How did you get him out of the federal headquarters?" Adam asked.

"First, I explained to him if he gave me a problem that I would shoot him. Then I blindfolded and gagged him, and after that I found my way out of the camp."

"Gray Ghost, that's a very interesting story. I know after the Union Army traded the fifty Confederate prisoners for him that he was released from military duty."

Mrs. Mosby had returned with the cup of hot tea. "It took longer than I figured. It was the last bag of tea in the house."

"John, I'm paying you five hundred dollars for this interview. I know dad would've wanted me to do that."

"Thank you, young man. I have many more stories anytime you want to come back and hear 'em. My civilian law practice didn't turn out so well."

"John, I'll say goodbye to you and Mrs. Mosby. It's been an honor meeting you. You've had an interesting life. I'll publish your story. Thanks again."

The next day a minor second page headline read, "Civil War Gray Ghost Found". The article recapped the capture of Gen. Stoughton. Thomas Horiska left the Mosbys a happier couple. They celebrated at dinner later that night.

Colonel John Singleton Mosby lived two years after that interview. Ah Pshaw, in 1916, at the age of eighty-three, the old square rooter crossed over the Potomac River to rest under the tree with me. All my friends have joined me now. I no longer have any desire to keep up with mortal happenings. We can now play again as we did at the Academy.

0-595-34479-8

Printed in the United States
27201LVS00006B/172-183

9 780595 344796